THE KING
FAMILY SAGA

An Amish Deception

AN AMISH ROMANCE

Jennifer Spredemann

BOOKS by JENNIFER SPREDEMANN

AMISH BY ACCIDENT TRILOGY
Englisch on Purpose
Amish by Accident
Christmas in Paradise

AMISH SECRETS SERIES
An Unforgivable Secret - 1
A Secret Encounter - 2
A Secret of the Heart - 3
An Undeniable Secret - 4
A Secret Sacrifice - 5
A Secret of the Soul - 6
A Secret Christmas - 7 (aka 2.5)

AMISH BIBLE ROMANCES
An Amish Reward
An Amish Deception
An Amish Honor
An Amish Blessing
An Amish Betrayal

AMISH COUNTRY BRIDES
The Trespasser
The Heartbreaker
The Charmer
The Drifter
The Giver
The Teacher
The Widower
The Keeper

The Pretender
The Arrangement (releasing 2022 in the Amish
Spring Romance collection)

UNLIKELY SERIES
Unlikely Santa
Unlikely Sweethearts
Unlikely Singing (More Amish Christmas
Miracles collection)

OTHER
The Princess and the Prayer Kapp (Amish Fairy Tale
2-in-1 Collection)
Learning to Love – Saul's Story (Sequel to Chloe's
Revelation – adult novella)
Her Amish Identity (formerly Love Impossible)
An Unexpected Christmas Gift (from the Amish
Christmas Miracles Collection)
The Arrangement (Amish Spring Romance collection)

BOOKS by J.E.B. SPREDEMANN
AMISH GIRLS SERIES
Joanna's Struggle
Danika's Journey
Chloe's Revelation
Susanna's Surprise
Annie's Decision
Abigail's Triumph
Brooke's Quest
Leah's Legacy
A Christmas of Mercy – Amish Girls Holiday

BOOKS by J.E.B. SPREDEMANN

AMISH GIRLS SERIES
Joanna's Struggle
Danika's Journey
Chloe's Revelation
Susanna's Surprise
Annie's Decision
Abigail's Triumph
Brooke's Quest
Leah's Legacy
A Christmas of Mercy – Amish Girls Holiday

BOOKS by BRANDI GABRIEL
The Orphan Bride
The Cowhand's Bride
If He Only Knew (co-authored with Michelynn Christy)

Unofficial Glossary
of Pennsylvania Dutch Words

Ab im kopp – Off in the head, crazy

Ach – Oh

Aldi – Girlfriend

Bann – Shunning

Boppli/Bopplin – Baby/Babies

Bruder – Brother

Daed/Dat – Dad

Dawdi – Grandfather

Dawdi Haus – A small house intended to house parents
    or grandparents

Denki – Thanks

Der Herr – The Lord

Dochder – Daughter

Dochter – Doctor

Dummkopp – Dummy

Ehemann – Husband

Englischer – A non-Amish person

Fraa – Wife

G'may – Members of an Amish fellowship

Gott – God

Grossdochder – Granddaughter

Mammi – Grandmother

Gut – Good

Jah – Yes

Kapp – Amish head covering

Kinner – Children

Mamm – Mom

(Gross)Mammi – Grandmother

Mei fraa – My wife

Ordnung – Rules of the Amish community

Rumspringa – Running around period for Amish youth

Schatzi – Sweetheart

Schweschder(n) – Sister(s)

Sehr gut – Very good

Wunderbaar – Wonderful

Dear Reader,

This series is loosely based on stories of actual people who are mentioned in the Bible. These books are not necessarily retellings, although you will find quite a few similarities between the books and their Bible counterparts. I am, in no way, attempting to rewrite the Bible (God has done a fine job with it and He certainly doesn't need my help!) nor am I depicting the true Biblical characters. The characters in my books are portrayed as Amish and there are some things contained in the actual Biblical accounts that simply cannot be included, due to Amish culture and customs. With that said, I hope that you will enjoy this series as it is, but I also hope that it will encourage you to go back and read the *actual* Bible stories themselves. There are so many truths contained in God's Word that we can never even really scratch the surface of its depth. His mercy and grace are beyond measure.

Blessings,
J. Spredemann

ONE

*J*acob shoveled a forkful of supper into his mouth and glanced up at his father who sat at the head of the table. Was he *humming*? How *Dat* loved his venison. And the son who'd hunted for it. A pang of jealousy cinched Jacob's heart.

One thing he'd always longed for was his father's approval—something he'd never had.

"*Ach*, this must be some of the best venison I've ever tasted!" *Dat* boasted. Jacob had heard this speech so many times he predicted *Dat's* next words. "Ephraim, you are one of the best hunters I've ever known."

"*Denki, Dat!*" His brother beamed at their father's praise. It seemed Ephraim could do no wrong. "I tried a new recipe this time."

Of course he did. Jacob sighed, clenching his hand in a fist.

His mother squeezed his other hand under the table.

"Jacob grew the vegetables," *Mamm* said.

Dat grunted. He couldn't care less about vegetables. The only reason he forced vegetables down his throat is because *Mamm* insisted he eat them to stay healthy.

"He should learn to hunt like his *bruder*. Ain't nothin' like venison stew."

Did Ephraim just sneer? He already knew what his brother thought of his gardening skills—it was women's work. Anyone could do it, he'd claimed. A *real* man hunted for his food, he'd insisted.

Jacob had always had a heart for animals, which is why he preferred not to kill them if he could help it. He'd much rather help *Dat* care for the horses on their ranch and assist *Mamm* with the gardening.

Dat had always favored Ephraim, although he'd never been intentionally cruel to Jacob. He supposed *Dat* still loved him in his own way. But not as much as Ephraim. Never as much as Ephraim.

And *Dat's* favoritism seemed to worsen the older he got.

"He also grew the lilacs. Don't they smell *wunderbaar*?" *Mamm* pointed to the vase on the table.

Dat shrugged. "*Jah*, the flowers are nice. Lilacs were my *mamm's* favorite." He offered an obligatory smile.

Well, that was *something*. Probably as closed to a compliment as Jacob would get.

He lifted his eyes to see his brother shaking his head and holding in a chuckle. His brother had an uncanny way of making him feel two inches tall. Well, he was sick and tired of his brother's condescending superiority complex. Pride was not their way. He wished Ephraim would be called out on it, but it was not Jacob's place.

Ephraim was literally one minute older than him, but he acted as though he were a decade his senior.

They'd have it out for sure. Eventually. He'd best his brother yet. He just had to be patient and wait for the perfect time. And patient was something he'd learned to be while tending to his garden. He could be patient.

Just wait and see, Ephraim.

Jacob ran a brush through the mane of one of their horses and thought back to his school days. He'd tried everything to gain his folks' approval. He knew that he'd always had *Mamm's*. She supported him in everything. But when it came to *Dat*, he always wanted to hear about what Ephraim had done during recess. It was as though Jacob's getting a high score on a test paled in comparison to Ephraim's home run.

His parents must've decided from early on that Jacob was *Mamm's* favorite and Ephraim was *Dat's*. As far back as he could remember, it had always been that way. Didn't they realize that children needed both a mother's and a father's attention?

He surveyed his folks as they walked hand-in-hand in the cool evening. Although they seemed to play favorites with their sons, it was clear to Jacob that his *mamm* and *dat* were deeply in love, even after being married all these years. Aside from *Der Herr*, no one on this earth was more important.

Jacob longed for that kind of relationship with a woman. What would it be like to find someone who looked at him the way *Mamm* looked at *Dat*—as though he were the most handsome, most important person in the whole world.

Ach, perhaps that was how he would gain his father's approval. Jacob knew good and well that neither *Mamm* nor *Dat* approved of Ephraim's choice of *maed*. Would he marry the *Englisch maedel* he'd been dating the last several months? She didn't share their views on hardly anything. Jacob figured his brother likely dated her because she allowed him to drive her fancy car. She was worldly. Not a woman Jacob would ever consider dating.

Jacob thought of the *maed* in their district. There seemed to be more *buwe* than *maed* his age. That was one of the reasons *Grossdawdi* and *Onkel* Ezekiel brought *Mamm* and *Aenti* Lucy here some years ago. There hadn't been enough *maed* to go around. *Jah*, he still had a chance. There were single *maed* available who would probably have him if he desired, but none of them had caught his eye. He wanted someone like *Mamm*.

TWO

" Hey, Jacob." Ephraim pulled up in a fancy sportscar that likely belonged to his *Englisch* girlfriend. He would stop at nothing to fulfill his lustful desires, it seemed.

Oh, no. What did his brother want now? "*Jah*?"

"I need to borrow some money. Badly."

"What for?"

"I can't tell you."

"*Nee*. You still haven't paid me back for the last couple of times you borrowed from me. Why don't you go ask *Dat*?"

Ephraim sneered. "Do you really expect *Dat* to give me more money?"

More money? *Ach*, *Dat* had never given Jacob any money. At least, he never gave him money he hadn't earned. Of course, he'd never asked for any either, so there was that.

"Come on. I'm serious. I need money. Now." Ephraim demanded.

"You don't have to be so pushy. What if I don't have any?"

"Oh, you have it alright. You're a tightwad, remember?"

"You know, you can catch more flies with honey than vinegar."

"Why on earth would I want to attract flies? You've got to be the *dummest bu* that ever lived."

Case in point.

Jacob frowned. "I'm not giving you money."

"C'mon, Jake. I'm desperate. It's a matter of life and death." His brother had always been overdramatic. Wasn't that what he'd said last time?

"What do you need it for?"

"I told you I couldn't say."

Frankly, Jacob was tired of being the nice guy. Especially since his *bruder* never appreciated his sacrifices. But he didn't have time to stand there and quarrel with his brother all day. "Fine. How much do you need?"

"Five hundred."

"Five hundred dollars?" He practically shouted the words.

"I promise I'll pay you back as soon as I can."

"When?"

8

"Our next birthday. Two weeks."

"You can't wait two weeks?" That was hard to believe.

"*Nee*. I told you I need it *now*."

"You're *really* going to pay me back? Is that a deal? A promise?"

"*Jah, jah*. Sure, whatever."

Jah, he'd heard that before. "What are you going to give me as collateral?"

"Collateral? What's that mean?"

"You know, you really should have paid more attention to your studies in school, instead of focusing on girls and sports."

"I don't need a lecture right now. I just need money."

"Fine. Where's the deed to *Dat's* property?"

"The deed? You mean the will?"

The one he was conveniently left out of? "*Jah*, that one."

"I'm not giving you that!"

"It's only until our birthday, remember? When you pay me back." Not that he actually would.

Ephraim shrugged. "I guess it's not going to do me any *gut* if I'm dead anyhow. It's in my room, in the top drawer of my dresser."

Jacob turned serious. Maybe his brother wasn't

joking. Maybe he was in grave trouble. "Ephraim, what's going on? You don't owe anybody drug money or anything, do you?"

Ephraim laughed, but it wasn't genuine.

Ach, he must be in some kind of trouble. *Gott, please help my bruder with whatever trouble he's gotten himself into this time.*

"You're lucky I just came from the bank." Jacob fished in his wallet and handed his twin brother the money he so desperately pled for. "Okay. You're paying me back. Don't forget."

Ephraim rolled his eyes, while tucking the money into his pocket. He jumped back into the fancy car and peeled out of their driveway, leaving Jacob in a plume of dust.

"Thanks a lot, *bruder*." Jacob coughed.

Ephraim wouldn't be paying him back, that much he knew. He'd be holding Ephraim to his promise, for sure and for certain.

"*Mamm*, I need your advice on something." Jacob yanked up another weed by the roots and tossed it into the wheelbarrow with the others he'd uprooted within the last hour.

"Does this have to do with your *bruder*?"

Jacob nodded and pulled the paper from his pocket. He handed it to his mother.

Her brow furrowed as she stared down at it. "Your *vatter's* will?"

"*Jah*. I took it from Ephraim's room."

"I don't understand. Why?"

"We had an agreement, you see. I loaned him quite a bit of money and he promised to pay it back. He never did. It's been several months now and every time I ask him, he shrugs me off." He grunted. "I don't think he has any intention of paying me back. I've already given him time."

"And the will?"

Jah, he still hadn't explained that part.

"We made a deal. If he didn't pay me back by our last birthday, he would forfeit his inheritance."

"He gave this to you then?"

"*Nee*, he wouldn't give it up. I had to take it from his room. But he promised me." Jacob's brow lowered. "What do you think?"

She shrugged. "A promise is a promise. What good is it if it isn't kept?"

"You think it is okay that I took it then?"

Mamm smiled. "It wonders me if my mother's intuition saw this coming. I made sure your father used an erasable pen to write the name on his will. You know that he was planning to leave most of everything to your *bruder*. It will all be his on his next birthday. But I will not stand for it.

"Your father may have confidence in him, but I do not. Ephraim is irresponsible and not fit to run this ranch. He will run it into the ground and likely leave us all homeless. *You* are the one who should rightly have it, Jacob. You would be diligent and care for it as you should. I love your father, but he was not thinking straight. We will make sure that you get the inheritance."

And that was part of his dilemma. "We will? But how? It still has Ephraim's name on it."

"I want you to change the name on this one and the one in your father's office when your father and I go out today. Erase your brother's name from the will and write in your name with a permanent pen. There are only two copies. It is a homemade will, but it would still hold up in court, if ever contested."

"*Ach, Mamm*. I don't think I can do that. *Dat* would be upset. And he will likely just tear it up and make a new will."

"*Nee*. I will handle your father. He will agree with me on this, once he sees things as they are."

"I feel bad deceiving him like this."

"You won't feel bad if your *bruder* inherits this land and it falls apart. Ephraim is unwise, He will squander all he is given."

"*Ach*, you are right."

"Trust me in this, *sohn*."

"Okay, I will." But if his father found out. Or worse yet, Ephraim… He didn't want to think of the consequences. Surely *Dat* and Ephraim would be upset.

"As soon as you do, I want you to go to the bank and put it in a safe deposit box. That way, it will not be easily accessible."

"*Jah*, okay." Jacob blew out a breath.

Although he felt just in what he was doing, guilt nibbled at him. If for nothing else, at least for usurping *Dat's* authority. It was not Jacob's place to do so and surely would be frowned upon by the leaders. But if even *Mamm* had agreed, why should he feel guilty? Ephraim had promised after all.

THREE

*E*phraim thrust the door wide, slamming it against the wall, and came storming out of the *haus*. "Alright, Jacob, where is it?" he shouted.

"Where's what?"

"Don't play *dumm*. You know exactly what I'm referring to."

"Can't say I do." He scratched his chin.

"The will." Ephraim said through gritted teeth. "Where is the will? My inheritance."

"Why do you want it now? What are you going to do with it?"

Was his brother going to do something *narrisch*, like put the ranch up for sale so he could buy himself a fancy sports car or a motorcycle? *Ach*, it was a bothersome thought for sure. But he wouldn't put it past his brother to do something so foolish. What Jacob lacked in hunting prowess, Ephraim lacked in intellect

15

and common sense. Sometimes, Jacob actually felt bad for his older brother.

"Is that any of your business? No, it is not. Just hand it over, Jacob. I want my inheritance," Ephraim demanded.

"Oh. I think you mean *my* inheritance."

"No. *Dat* promised it to *me*."

"And *you* promised it to *me*, remember?"

"I did no such thing!"

The liar. "You did. Remember the money I loaned you? The money you never paid back?"

"You're still crying about that?"

"A promise is a promise. I kept up my end. Now you're keeping yours too. I'll make an honest man out of you yet."

Apparently, Ephraim hadn't like that answer. "Honest? You stole *Dat's* will and my inheritance!"

Jacob wished he'd seen what was coming next, but it was too late to block his brother's punch. As he doubled over, his brother charged him full speed ahead and knocked him to the ground, delivering blow after blow. But Jacob was a *gut*, faithful Amish man. He refused to fight his *bruder*, but he attempted to protect himself against Ephraim's fury.

"Ephraim!" *Mamm* shrieked as she dropped a basket of laundry on the ground and rushed toward the tumult. "*Nee*! Jacob!"

One of their hired hands rushed toward Ephraim and Jacob. He grabbed Ephraim's suspenders and hoisted him off the ground, separating him from Jacob.

Jacob moaned and spit dust from his mouth. *Ach*, he was certain he had some broken ribs at the least.

"Jacob, you're hurt!" *Mamm* cried. "Dear, *Gott*, let him be okay."

At *Mamm's* words, Ephraim left off in a sprint toward the barn. A moment later, the sound of tires squealing met their ears.

Hopefully, Ephraim wouldn't be back anytime soon. Jacob would pray for that.

He attempted to rise, but the pain was too great. He sunk back to the ground. His eyes draped shut, seemingly against his will.

Beep. Beep. Beep. Beep.

Jacob startled awake.

"Shh…lie still, *sohn*." He recognized the voice. *Dat*?

He slowly took in his surroundings. A thin white blanket covered his body as he lay on a narrow bed with rails on each side. Some sort of device had been strapped to his hand. As he moved it, a sharp pain resulted. That was when he noticed something sticking to the top of his hand. It was connected to a transparent tube with clear liquid inside, that meandered upward to a bag holding the liquid. It hung from a metal stand.

Images flashed from a television in the corner, but the volume was turned low.

He gaze flickered to his father, who quietly observed him.

Jacob sat up. "Ugh…" he moaned as excruciating pain shot through his middle.

"*Nee, sohn*. The *dochter* said you must lie still."

Ach, this whole situation was confusing. Was he having a bad dream?

"What…why am I here? Where am I?" Jacob frowned. He didn't like this. He wanted to move.

"You're at the hospital, *sohn*. You and your brother had a disagreement." *Dat's* eyes narrowed.

"A disagreement?"

"About the will…" *Ach*, Jacob read the disappointment in *Dat's* eyes. He loathed that look, but it was a familiar one. For once, he wished he could gain *Dat's* approval. See the same look of admiration and appreciation *Dat* often bestowed on Jacob's twin brother.

"I'm sorry, *Dat*. I was wrong. If you want to change it back—"

Dat shook his head. "*Nee*. What's done is done. It is *Der Herr's* will."

Really? Ach, this is not the reaction he'd expected out of *Dat.*

"I *am* disappointed in your trickery, Jacob. Deception does not become you." He rubbed his chin. "But I can see that this would be best. With your brother's actions lately…" *Dat* shook his head.

Could it be he was disappointed in Ephraim too?

"Let this…" *Dat* gestured to the hospital bed. "Be a lesson to you."

"*Jah*, I will." He swallowed. "*Denki, Dat.*"

Dat reached over and squeezed his hand. "*Ich liebe dich, sohn.*" He stood and walked out of the room.

Jacob stared after his father, his mouth agape in wonder. That had gone better than he could have ever imagined.

"*Ach, denki, Gott!*" he whispered.

FOUR

After spending several long days in the hospital, Jacob felt *gut* to be back in his comfortable log cabin home. The doctor had said it would be many weeks before he completely recovered from some of his injuries, mainly his fractured ribs, but they'd done all they could for him at the hospital. He'd also sustained a concussion and extensive bruising, which were both well on their way to healing.

Every movement, it seemed, brought pain. He remembered *Dat's* words of warning, *let this be a lesson to you*. And a painful lesson it had been.

Fortunately, he hadn't seen Ephraim at all. He guessed his folks likely forbid him to go near Jacob. At least, that was what he hoped. Because if Ephraim came at him now, there'd be no way for him to defend himself.

Guilt flooded Jacob as he thought of all the work that

21

would fall on *Mamm's* and *Dat's* shoulders, now that he was laid up. Perhaps Ephraim would be called to step up to the plate more often.

Which would only fuel his hatred for Jacob. He sighed.

Jah, he'd been wrong.

"Jacob, may I *kumm* in?" *Mamm* called to him from the other side of his bedroom door.

"*Jah*."

She marched in and pulled the door shut.

Jacob's brow furrowed. What was so urgent?

"I found this in your *bruder's* things." She held out a notebook.

Jacob glanced down at the writing on the page. It appeared to be a journal of some sort. It was clearly his brother Ephraim's handwriting.

"Read it." His mother insisted.

Ach, he hated to delve into his brother's personal items. Ephraim was already so upset. But *Mamm* seemed adamant.

His eyes focused on the words in front of him.

I hate Jacob. I've hated him ever since we were little and he turned Mamm against me. As soon as Dat passes away, I will see that Jacob gets what he deserves. Maybe sooner yet. He will not get away with what he's done

Jacob frowned, then looked at his mother.

"He has been very angry lately and only speaks evil of you. I don't like to even think this, but I suspect he might be planning to do something really bad. Worse than the injuries you've just recovered from. Maybe even kill you, Jacob. Nothing good can come of your brother's anger."

Jacob had barely resumed his duties working on the ranch. He despised the prospect of being laid up yet again. Perhaps even worse than his first stint in the hospital. He groaned at the very thought of it.

"What should I do?"

"I found this a few days ago. I phoned my cousin in Pennsylvania and she agreed to help you. I've also called a driver for you. He will take you to the bus station. The bus will take you close to the community where I grew up, then you can call Jim. He's one of the family's drivers. I have a few distant relatives there—they're related to your Aunt Lucy—and they will take you in."

Wait. What? Jacob's head spun. He had to leave? Pennsylvania? "What about *Dat*? Does he know? What does he say about this?"

"He's in agreement, but he doesn't know about what Ephraim wrote. He does not want you to find a *fraa* here. You know how much grief Ephraim's *Englisch maedel* has caused us. He doesn't want the same fate for you. My cousin says there are many nice *maed* in the community. More *maed* than young men, so you'll likely have your pick." *Mamm* smiled. "You will find a nice *fraa*."

"But I'll have to leave you and *Dat*? I think I might regret changing the will and taking Ephraim's inheritance. I know that's mostly why Ephraim hates me so." He pressed his lips together in a frown. "Maybe we should try to change the will back."

"*Nee*, Jacob. Just let it be. Ephraim will eventually get over himself. He just needs time. Come back after you've found a *fraa*. This ranch belongs to you now. It will be a wonderful *gut* place to raise your *kinner*."

Jacob swallowed. "Okay, *jah*. I will do what you think is best, *Mamm*."

"Your father and I are in agreement on this. *Der Herr's* hand of blessing will go with you. We will miss you for sure and for certain, but it is time to make your own way. Away from your brother's threats."

"You will keep in touch then?"

"*Jah*, I will write you as often as I can. Do not worry about us. We will be fine."

24

FIVE

*J*acob tapped his fingers on his broadfall trousers. *Ach*, how many more hours until they arrived at their destination? Fortunately, he'd been told this was the final leg of his journey.

He was ready for this road trip to be over with. He just wanted to get settled into wherever he was going and acclimate to his new surroundings as soon as possible.

"Wow, look at that sunset! Isn't it amazing?"

Jacob angled his head to where his driver motioned. "*Jah*, it's nice."

"Man, it just makes me wonder what Heaven's gonna be like. You know?"

He shrugged, not really feeling the man's enthusiasm. "I reckon."

"I mean, think about it, Jake. If God made this world and all its beauty in six days, just imagine how

Heaven's going to look after He's been working on it for over two thousand years."

Jacob twisted his lips. What was Larry talking about? "Two thousand years?"

"Yeah. Before Jesus left this earth, He said He was going to prepare a place for His followers. That was over two thousand years ago." He shook his head, a grin stretched wide across his face. "I can just see myself walking on those streets of gold, talking with Jesus. Man, it's going to be awesome."

This man was talking as though he *knew* that he was going to be in Heaven. Like it was an already established fact. And he was *Englisch*. How could this *Englischer* sound so sure of his place in Heaven and that he would meet Jesus? He drove this fancy worldly vehicle. His clothes were worldly. His music was worldly. His cell phone was worldly.

Surely, Larry was deceiving himself. His brazen attitude smacked of *hochmut*. Pride. And it was downright sinful, to Jacob's thinking.

"Don't you agree?"

Jacob shrugged. "I don't know about all that."

"What do you mean? You're Amish, right? Don't Amish follow the Bible?"

"*Jah*, we do."

"So?"

"We do not believe a man can know that he is going to Heaven. It is prideful to think that you are good enough. We will not know if we are good enough until we stand in front of *Gott*."

"Is that what you believe?"

"Well, *jah*. *Hochmut*, pride, is a sin, ain't not?"

"Jake, I think you've misunderstood me. I can *never ever* be good enough to get to Heaven. I can do all the good works in the world and it will never be enough."

"Why not?"

"Because God said so. That is not how a person gets into Heaven. That's not the measuring stick God uses. The Bible says '*Not by works of righteousness which we have done, but according to his mercy he saved us, by the washing of regeneration, and the renewing of the Holy Ghost.*' It also says that *our righteousnesses are as filthy rags.*'

The driver glanced toward him, likely getting the message that what he'd just said had gone right over his head. "Are you following me?"

Jacob shook his head. "*Nee.*"

Larry explained. "You see, the Bible says that you must be born again. *Except a man be born again, he cannot see the kingdom of God.* That is what it means by regeneration. It is like you get a brand-new life, a spiritual one. Until we are born again, the Bible says that we are dead in trespasses and sins." He looked at him. "Do you understand?"

"I think so."

He nodded. "The thing is, you must place your trust in Jesus, because He is the only one who can save you. When you accept the payment Jesus gave on the cross—His perfect blood sacrifice—His blood washes away all your sins, and you receive eternal life."

"I believe in Jesus. I mean, I've read about what He did. When He died."

"But have you received Him? It is one thing to know about Jesus with your head, but it's an entirely different matter to believe from your heart. When you believe from your heart, God does something wonderful."

"What do you mean?"

"Well, besides cleansing you from your sins and giving you everlasting life—which are wonderful in themselves—Jesus comes to live inside your heart. He changes you from the inside out. He gives you a desire to do His will. He gives you understanding when you read His Word."

"Are you a preacher?"

He chuckled. "No, not in an official sense. But God has called each of His children to share the Gospel. Do you know what the Gospel is?"

"The story of Jesus?"

"That's part of it. But the Bible describes the Gospel like this, *That Christ died for our sins according to the Scriptures; and that he was buried, and that he rose again the third day according to the Scriptures.* He wants all men to be saved. And that includes you and your people, Jake."

"But this is not how I was taught. I must keep the traditions of my forefathers."

"You can keep your traditions. You don't have to give those up. You see, it is not the horse and buggy that saves you. That reminds me of a verse in the Old Testament. *Some trust in chariots and some in horses, but we will remember the name of the Lord our God.*

"Jacob, it is not the clothes, or how you plow your fields. Salvation comes through Jesus, and through Him alone. It really is that simple. The only way you'd need to give up a tradition is if it contradicts—goes against—God's Word."

"How do I know if it does?"

"Well, you'd need to study God's Word so you know what it says."

"Does it say anything about being Plain?"

"Not directly. Does everyone in your church believe that they have to be Amish to be saved?"

"I do not know. Our leaders do not teach on being saved. That is a prideful *Englisch* teaching. They teach us to live like we know we should, to obey our authorities. Then we can have hope of Heaven. When someone jumps the fence, we urge them to return so they won't be in danger of hell fire."

"Why would they be in danger of hell fire?"

"For forsaking our ways, for disobeying their parents and their leaders, for not continuing in the path *Der Herr*—the Lord—has laid out for them."

"Do you remember what I just quoted to you? The verses about believing in Jesus to be saved?"

"*Jah.*"

"Do you know John three sixteen?"

Jacob frowned. "I know I've heard it, but I'm not sure exactly how it goes."

"*For God so loved the world that he gave his only begotten Son, that whosoever believeth in him should not perish, but have everlasting life.*"

"I remember now."

"Think about those words, Jake. The Bible doesn't say anything about needing to be Amish or even have good works to get into Heaven. As a matter of fact, over and over again, the Bible states that salvation is *not* of works. Jesus did the work for us when He died on the cross. That is why we must believe." He reached over and opened up the glove box, keeping his eyes on the road. "Grab my Bible out of there, would ya?"

Jacob nodded and took his Bible from the glove box.

"Now, turn to the book of Romans."

Jacob stared at him blankly. Where on earth was Romans? "Is that in the New Testament?"

"Yeah, open it about three quarters of the way."

He did as instructed, then looked up at the heading on the page. "Colossians."

"Okay, turn back several pages."

He did.

"Okay, there. Turn to chapter ten, I think, then read it."

He turned to the suggested place, feeling somewhat uneasy. Would the leaders be okay with him reading the Bible with an *Englischer*? He'd heard warnings about *Englischers* leading people astray, causing some to jump the fence. That was why they discouraged studying the Bible in depth. You might misinterpret something and it would lead you away from the *g'may*.

"Did you find it?"

"*Jah*." He swallowed, then looked down at the words. *"Brethren, my heart's desire and prayer to God for Israel is, that they might be saved."*

"Okay, that's the Apostle Paul speaking. He was Jewish, or an Israelite. He wanted so badly for his people to be saved, but for the most part, Israel as a nation rejected Jesus, their messiah." He pointed to the

31

Bible Jacob held. "Go ahead and read the next few verses."

"For I bear them record that they have a zeal of God, but not according to knowledge.

For they being ignorant of God's righteousness, and going about to establish their own righteousness, have not submitted themselves unto the righteousness of God.

For Christ is the end of the law for righteousness to every one that believeth."

"Do you understand that?"

"Not really."

"Okay, so Paul was a Jew originally named Saul. Saul was a devout Jew. He would do anything to uphold and protect the Jewish religion, even to the point of sending those who believed in Jesus to prison and to their deaths. He was the real deal."

"He would hurt people because of his religion?"

Larry nodded. "I know, it sounds crazy, but yes. He felt like Jesus and His followers were a direct threat to his religion, so he persecuted them. But that was only until Jesus met him on the road to Damascus. He was en route to imprison more Christians until he was blinded by God. You see, God knew Saul's heart. His heart was in the right place, but he was ignorant. He was fighting *against* God and he didn't even know it.

And that is what Paul is talking about in those verses."

Jacob nodded. Larry's words made sense.

"See, God's way is not by our works, it is through the work that Jesus did for us on the cross. It is His work that is good enough to get us into Heaven. And that is what Paul was trying to get Israel to see. They were establishing their own righteousness—their own rules or *Ordnung*, if you will—but they were ignorant of what could truly help them—God's righteousness, which could only be obtained through believing in Jesus Christ."

"Do you...do you think that is what my Amish church is doing?"

"It doesn't matter what I think, Jake. What matters is what that book says. God is not a liar. He shoots straight with us." Larry frowned. "But if you're being taught something different than what you just read in that book, there's a good chance someone is steering you in the wrong direction."

Jacob stared at Larry. He had so many questions. "So you think that leaving the Amish church—not that I would—will *not* send me to hell?"

"Hell ain't got one whit to do with the Amish church. The only thing that sends people to hell is unbelief—or trusting in something other than Jesus for salvation. Jesus is the way, the truth, and the life. He is the only one who can wash away your sins. He is the *only* way to Heaven. If you have trusted in something else, you have not submitted yourself to the righteousness of God. It does not matter which religion you're from or if you have no religion at all. What do you believe about Christ? Have *you* received Him as *your* Saviour?"

"Are you asking *me*?"

"I wasn't necessarily asking you, but the question applies to every person."

"I don't really know what to do." He shrugged. "How do I submit to the righteousness of God?"

"Basically, you just acknowledge that Jesus is the only one who can get you into Heaven. Ask Him to forgive your sins and save you. Believe with your whole heart."

"And that's it?"

"Yep, that's all that's required to be saved. Look at Romans chapter ten again and now read verses nine through thirteen. You don't have to read it out loud."

Jacob looked down at the page in the Bible and read the verses quietly. He looked up at Larry. "*Ach*, how do you know so much about this book?"

"*Study to show thyself approved unto God, a workman that needeth not to be ashamed, rightly dividing the word of truth*. It's in Second Timothy chapter two. I love God's Word and He's given me a desire to know what it says. I want to study it so I can know God's mind in whatever situation comes my way."

Jacob frowned. How different Larry's mindset was from what he'd been taught his whole life—that studying the Bible too much would make one prideful. Yet, Larry didn't seem prideful about his knowledge, he seemed sincere.

"So what are you gonna do, Jake? Are you going to ask Jesus to save you?"

He shrugged. "I guess I need to think on it for a little bit."

"Well, don't think on it too long. I'd hate for us to get in a car wreck and have you die not knowing whether you'd be in Heaven or not."

Ach, when Larry put it that way... Jacob squeezed his eyes shut. *Gott, if what Larry is saying is the truth, I want to be saved. I want to know that I am going to Heaven and that my sins are forgiven. Denki. Amen.*

SIX

"**W**ell, it looks like we're here." Larry pointed to a decent sized farmhouse as they drove up a driveway. "I'm gonna miss seeing you around, Jake. What a coincidence that I happened to be going this way the same time you needed a ride. Saved your folks some bus fare, no doubt. I'll check in with your folks now and then to ask about you, so be sure to write or call them."

"*Jah*, I will." Jacob took a deep breath. "*Denki*, Larry, for talking to me about Jesus."

"When the Holy Spirit nudges me, it's hard to keep my mouth shut." He laughed. "I'm just glad you listened."

He smiled. "Me too. Maybe it wasn't a coincidence, ain't so?" He fished into his wallet and paid Larry for his services. "Have a safe ride home."

"Do you need help unloading?"

"Nah, I just have a couple of things. You could probably stay for supper."

"Thanks for the invite, but I'd like to get back home sooner rather than later. Hey, wait a sec. Why don't you take my Bible?" He handed it to him.

Ach, he felt like he'd been given a *wunderbaar gut* gift. "*Denki*."

"You'll read it, won't you?"

"*Jah*, I'll read it." But he'd need to stuff it into his suitcase so no one would see it. He didn't want to get on the *g'may's* bad side before he even got to know anybody. Carrying a Bible around was not something one did in their community. *Nee*, the Bible was kept in the home, usually in a special place with other important books.

"See ya, Jake."

Jacob waved goodbye to his *Englisch* driver. He was ready to begin a new chapter in his life. At least this chapter included a real relationship with *Der Herr*. What did *Gott* have planned for him?

"Jacob King?" A man's voice called as he headed toward the house.

"*Jah*, it's me." He looked at the man, determining who he might be.

"I'm your *Onkel* Peter. Well, not really your uncle. Somewhere down the line, I guess we're related. Your

Aenti Lucy was my *fraa's* second cousin through marriage."

Ach, he had no idea how that all worked out. He did know the *Aenti* Lucy was *Mamm's dat, Grossdawdi* Benuel's, *schweschder*, though. Somehow, these folks were kin. "*Gut* to meet you."

"Let's get you inside. Fannie and the girls should have supper on soon. I hope you're hungry."

"I can always eat." Jacob followed him inside. He stood awkwardly near the back door, holding his bags, while his uncle washed up in the mudroom.

"*Kumm*. I'll introduce you to everyone." His uncle left his boots in the mudroom and walked toward the kitchen in his socks.

"Should I take my boots off?"

"*Nee*, only if they're dirty. I don't reckon you've been workin' much today."

Jacob chuckled. "*Nee*. Not at all."

"Cousin Jacob has arrived," his uncle announced as they entered the kitchen. "Jacob, this is *mei fraa*, Fannie. Our *dochdern*, Christy Ann, Jenny Lee, Mary Lynn, and the little one is Emma SuAnn."

Just then, the boys came skidding into the room. His uncle continued. "And this is Junior, Nathan, Phillip, and our oldest *bu* is Jeriah. He's nearest your age."

"*Gut* to meet you all, although I'm certain you'll

have to tell me your names again more than once." He grinned and nodded to Jeriah. Hopefully the two of them could become friends.

"Well, supper's about ready," Aenti Fannie declared as she sat a steaming dish on the table. "Has everyone washed up?" She carefully eyed the two youngest *buwe*.

"Junior didn't," the second youngest bu—was his name Phillip or was that Nathan?—volunteered.

"Did too, Nate."

"Not after you picked your nose!"

"Well, you didn't wash yours after you brought the frog in our room."

The other boy pressed his lips together and squinted at his younger brother, as though he had just committed an act of treason.

"Boys, there will be no wild animals, insects, reptiles, or amphibians in this *haus*. Do I make myself clear?" *Aenti* Fannie's hand planted on her hip and waited for their response. "And you both hurry up and wash your hands."

"Uh oh." Jacob frowned down at one of the suitcases still in his hand. "I guess I'll have to keep my pet snake in the barn then." He turned and winked at the boys.

The two youngest *buwe* stopped in their tracks and stared at him in wide-eyed admiration.

"Jacob King, you'd better be tellin' a tall tale." *Aenti* Fannie shook her finger.

"I actually don't care much for snakes, although I hear they're *gut* eatin'." He smiled.

His aunt released a relieved sigh, but Junior and Nathan were sorely disappointed.

"Jeriah." *Onkel* Peter pointed to Jacob. "Why don't you show Jacob upstairs to his room so he can leave his things in there. "Quickly."

Jeriah nodded and offered to carry one of Jacob's bags.

Jacob grinned his appreciation. The bags weren't exactly heavy, but he was ready to divest himself of them.

"That would be great." Jacob followed his cousin up the stairs.

"How long will you be staying here?" He pushed the door open to the first bedroom. Two twin size beds were inside. "You'll be sharing my room with me."

Jacob hated to impose. "I hope you don't mind. I know it's an inconvenience."

His cousin shrugged. "*Ach*, it is what it is. You'll likely be better company than Phillip." He eyed him. "Why are you here, anyway?"

Heat rose in Jacob's chest. Better to give *Mamm's* reason than the real one. The last thing he wanted was for the people of the *g'may* here to think he was greedy. Not many folks would look well to a man stealing his brother's inheritance.

Jacob chuckled. "My *mamm's* hoping I'll find a *fraa*."

Jeriah tossed his head back and laughed. "*Jah*, I think my *mamm's* hoping the same thing for me to get me out of her hair."

"How old are you?"

"Just twenty. You?"

"Twenty-three."

"I can see why your *mamm* is anxious to get you married off. My *mamm* would not stand to have me in the *haus* at twenty-four either. She and *Dat* married when *Dat* was twenty-two, so she expects each of her sons to be gone by then."

"What about your *schweschdern*?"

"It's even worse for them. No older than twenty-one. Christy Ann is nineteen, but she's got a beau." He shook his head. "*Mamm* and *Dat* don't want them to end up like one of our cousins, poor Leah Schmidt."

Jacob frowned. There weren't any *alt maed* in his district that he could think of. *Nee*, every eligible *maedel* had been married off since there seemed to be more *buwe* than *maed*. He felt sorry for this young woman—Leah, was it?—that folks used as a measuring stick. He briefly wondered if she knew how folks gossiped about her marital status behind her back.

"How old is she?"

"Leah?" Jeriah frowned. "Older than you. Likely twenty-six or so. Interested?"

Jacob held up his hands. "Hey, I just got here. I'm not quite ready to get married off just yet. I haven't even met any of the *maed* yet. Will she be at the singing?"

"*Nee*, she no longer attends the young folks' gatherings."

"Why not? I'd think if she's looking for an *ehemann*, she'd be present."

"*Nee*, everyone already knows her. She's the school teacher. If she was going to get hitched, I reckon she would've by now."

Well, he guessed that made sense.

"*Kumm, Mamm's* waiting on us."

"*Jah*, I'm starving."

"What do you say we go out back and play a game of corn hole after supper and chores?"

"Sounds *gut*." Jacob smiled. "But I bet I'll beat you."

Jeriah scoffed. "We'll see about that, cousin."

SEVEN

Jacob didn't think he'd be nervous attending the young folks' gathering, but it turned out he was. There were so many strangers, so many unfamiliar faces. His heart ached for the familiarity of home.

"Do you like to play baseball?" Jeriah gestured to the field where several of the *youngie*, both men and women played.

"I'm not that great at it, but I do enjoy playing."

"Nothing wrong with playing for enjoyment. Besides, I wouldn't take you for an expert after witnessing your demise in our corn hole competition."

"I didn't do *that* bad. Besides, you forget whose team I was on."

Jeriah chuckled. "Don't blame Nate. He did better than you did."

"Thanks a lot, cousin."

"Hey, I'm just speaking the truth."

Jacob shook his head. "Whatever."

"Let's play, then?"

"Sure."

"I'll just make sure we're on opposite teams." He lightly punched his shoulder.

Jacob clenched his heart. "You wound me."

By glint in Jeriah's eye, he knew Jacob was teasing. "Grab a mitt, I'll introduce you to everyone."

Jacob followed his cousin to the field.

"Hey, everyone, this is my cousin Jacob King. Jacob, this is everyone."

Jacob raised a hand. "Hi, everyone."

"You any good at hitting?" One of the young men held out a bat to him.

Jacob shrugged. He honestly didn't know if he was any good or not. He'd pretty much always tried to stay out of his brother's way. If they played together, he'd always let his brother win to avoid a temper tantrum. But now that Ephraim wasn't here, well, he didn't have any reason not to try. "I'll do my best."

The young man chuckled. "That doesn't sound too promising."

Jacob tried a few air swings with the bat.

"You're up!" The guy said.

Jacob stepped up to the plate. He let the first few pitches fly by. *Please help me, Lord.*

"Strike one!"

He turned and frowned at the umpire.

"Swing batter, batter, batter!" Someone from the opposing team called.

He eyed the next ball. The pitch came quickly, but he swung too soon.

"Strike two!"

Please, Lord. I really don't want to look like a loser in front of my new friends.

He took a deep breath, closing his eyes for a split second, then retightened his grip on the bat. The ball came fast again, just like the last one.

He swung with all his might.

The wooden bat fractured in his hands with a loud crack, and the ball went flying over the centerfielder's outstretched glove.

"Woo hoo!" One of his teammates called. "Run, Jacob, run!"

He dropped the bat, shot out of home plate, and ran with all his might, easily passing first, second, and third.

"It's coming! Slide, Jacob!" His cousin called out from the opposite team.

"Hey, don't root for him!" One of Jeriah's teammates chided.

"He's my cousin."

Jacob slid into home base the same time the ball landed in the catcher's mitt.

"Safe!" The umpire cried out, crossing his hands over each other in front of him then out to the sides.

Jacob's team cheered, along with several fans sitting along the sidelines. The other team protested.

"Great hit, Jacob!" Jeriah hollered from his shortstop position. "I'm picking your team next time."

Jeriah's teammates complained at his comment. He lifted his hands. "What? I want to be on the winning team."

Someone handed Jacob a bottle of water as he neared and sat in the dugout with his other team members. They each high-fived him. *Ach*, it felt *gut* to be accepted, admired. He bowed his head. *Denki, Gott.*

It had been his first homerun ever. Surely *Der Herr* was giving him favor in this new community.

EIGHT

Rachel Schmidt couldn't deny that she'd noticed the newcomer. *Ach*, who *wouldn't* notice handsome Jacob King? He was likely the most attractive boy—*nee*, man—she'd ever seen.

But there was something about him she didn't trust. She couldn't exactly pinpoint what it was. Perhaps it was the fact that he'd arrived in their community alone. What kind of Amish boy lives a solitary life? Where was his family? Why did he not wish to be around them? Was he running away from something? Or someone? Perhaps a former *aldi*?

She didn't think he was an imposter or anything. *Nee*, his accent and speech assured her Jacob King was Amish through and through.

Ach, maybe she was prejudging too much. He certainly had his reasons, whatever they were.

Her friend Judy nudged her. "*Mei vatter* said he's related to you."

Rachel's brow arched high. *Ach*, she would have remembered if she'd ever met Jacob King. He didn't possess a face she was likely to forget. And those eyes...solemn, brooding. *Ach*...

"Jeriah said your aunt was his *mamm's* second cousin, or something like that." Judy shrugged. "Which, I think that would make him your third cousin, ain't so?"

"*Ach*, I have no idea. Which aunt?"

"Your *Aenti* Fannie, I think?"

"She is my aunt only through marriage."

"Well, that's a *gut* thing, because he seems to have an eye for *you*."

"He...he does?" Rachel briefly glanced his way, then smoothed back the imaginary strand of hair that may have fallen from her *kapp*.

"*Ach*, he's staring at you, Rachel. For sure and certain, he'll want to take you for a ride in his carriage."

Fire spread through her face, warming her neck and ears. *Nee*, a boy as handsome as Jacob King couldn't be interested in her. "But he's a stranger. I have no idea what I'd say. I don't know anything about him."

"That's why you'd talk to him on your buggy ride. Ask him lots of questions."

"He looks quite a bit older than me, ain't so? What if he's *ferhoodled*?"

"He doesn't look *ferhoodled*. And if he is, just be yourself. A ride won't last a week. Just one night. I could think of what *I* might do with one night alone with Jacob King." A cunning smile stretched across Judy's face.

Rachel's jaw dropped and she stared at her bold friend. Judy was a year older, so she'd had much more experience riding in boys' buggies. She hadn't been secretive about her courting adventures by any means. At least, not among her closest friends. Judy had kissed at least half a dozen of the boys present. She'd once told Rachel that she wanted to marry the boy who kissed the best so she'd never tire of it.

Ach, what *would* a kiss from Jacob King be like? Did people even get tired of kissing?

Which had reminded Rachel of her *grossmammi's* words, "Kissin' don't last. It might make him smile for a moment or two, but a man will appreciate a *maedel* who can make his stomach smile till the day he dies."

Strange word pictures had always popped up into Rachel's head when *Mammi* said such things. She visualized smiling stomachs and lips falling off. Why wouldn't kissing last? She couldn't imagine getting tired of something so romantic and intimate as a kiss. And she'd never seen anyone without lips, so they obviously didn't fall off.

But she was too nervous to even dream about kissing Jacob King.

Jacob couldn't seem to take his eyes off the young woman across the yard. *Ach*, she was the sweetest thing he'd ever laid his eyes on. Beautiful, but she apparently had no idea judging by her bashfulness. Shy and innocent, yet she'd glanced his way more than once, planting a seed of hope that maybe, just maybe, she might agree to a ride with him.

He slightly nudged his cousin, Jeriah. After *Mamm* had sent a letter on behalf of Jacob, Jeriah's family had taken him in with open arms. Although he'd only arrived a few days ago, he'd already been given a position in *Onkle* Peter's flooring shop and was making decent money. Before too long, he'd be able to get a place of his own.

"Who is that?" Jacob asked his cousin.

"Who?" Jeriah followed his line of vision. "*Ach*, Rachel? Rachel Schmidt. She's our cousin." He grinned. "Do you want to meet her?"

Jah, he wanted to meet her alright. "A cousin?"

"Don't worry. Not closely related enough to

matter." He cuffed his arm. "She's perty, ain't so?"

"*Jah*, she is. *Sehr schee*." Jacob paused. "Schmidt sounds familiar."

"*Ach*, that's because I told you about her *schweschder*, Leah. The *alt maedel*." Jeriah began walking in Rachel's direction, then glanced back at him. "*Kumm*. She won't bite." He winked.

Maybe not, but was he ready? He blew out a breath and willed his pulse to slow down. "*Jah*, okay."

He followed his cousin near the chairs where Rachel sat with a friend. A game of volleyball ensued about twenty feet from the chairs.

Jacob felt a little out of place since he knew no one here except his cousins Jeriah, Christy Ann, and Jenny Lee, whom he'd only met a few days ago.

"Judy, Rachel, I'd like to introduce you to my cousin from Kentucky." Jeriah grinned like the Cheshire cat, pushing Jacob in their direction.

"Hello." The girls smiled. Rachel briefly glanced up, then stared at her hands.

He smiled, still unable to look away from beautiful Rachel.

Jeriah elbowed him. "Tell them your name."

"Oh, uh, I'm…I'm…" All coherent thought took flight with the volleyball someone had just served over the net.

Jeriah laughed. "Jacob King. And apparently he's lost his ability to speak."

Jacob shook his head, then chuckled. "*Jah*, Jacob."

Ach, he was a *dummkopp* for sure. Rachel would likely not give him the time of day.

"Rachel, why don't you show Jacob where the snack table is?" Jeriah prompted.

"Uh, *jah*. Okay." She glanced at Jacob, tucking her lower lip under her teeth. Was she nervous too, or just ruffled because Jeriah had put her on the spot?

"You don't have to," Jacob said, frowning. But what if she got the idea that he wasn't interested? *Ach*… "I mean, if you don't want to."

"No, she wants to," her friend—what was her name?—said.

Jah, they definitely needed to get away from their friends. Poor Rachel had turned three shades of pink, but she was lovely nonetheless.

They strolled slowly toward the house. "Where are you from?" Rachel flashed a shy smile.

"Kentucky. Northern Kentucky. Bishop Peachy's district."

She nodded. "I've never been to Kentucky. Is it nice?"

"*Jah*. It's lush and green and *wunderbaar*. We have a large horse ranch. Do you like horses?"

"*Jah*, they are *schee*. I usually tend to my father's sheep."

He nodded. "*Mei Mamm* keeps goats. She uses the milk to make soap."

"I'd like to try her soap sometime. I bet it leaves your hands soft."

He rubbed his hands together, itching to let her take hold of them. "I don't think it makes much difference when you work hard. But I wouldn't know either way because I've never used anything else."

"Do you mind?" She reached for his hand.

Ach… He didn't need any more invitation. He shook his head and held his hand out to her.

She gently rubbed her fingertips over his palms, then the top of his hand, causing all sorts of inexplicable sensations. *Ach*, he didn't think he could ever tire of Rachel's touch.

"They are softer, but I can still tell you are a hard worker."

Jah, he was a hard worker. He was working hard at breathing at this moment. He boldly curved his fingers around hers.

Her gaze shot to his face, surprise lit her expression. But she didn't take her hand away.

Although reluctant, he set her hand free. No need to scare her off before he even got a chance to court her.

"Sorry. I…I couldn't help myself."

Her smile indicated she didn't seem to mind. "Do you like it here?"

"I've only been here a few days, but *jah*. I like it so far." *Especially you. I like you. A lot.* But he wouldn't utter those words aloud. He'd scare her off for sure and certain then.

"*Gut*."

"Have you lived in this area your whole life?"

"*Jah*. I live with my *Dat* and older *schweschder*. My *mamm* died a couple of years ago."

"I'm sorry." He frowned. *Ach*, he couldn't imagine losing *Mamm*. "Were you close to her?"

"We had a *gut* relationship."

"Do you have any other siblings besides your sister?"

"*Nee*. What about you?" She handed him a paper bowl.

"I only have one *bruder*. We're twins, actually, but we don't look anything alike." He reached into one of the large bowls of popcorn with his bowl and filled it.

A smile spread across her face. "I always wanted to be a twin. Is it fun? Are you two best friends?"

Hardly. He tried to suppress a frown. It was anything *but* fun. "*Nee*, not at all. It's kind of a long story, but we've never been *gut* friends." He offered her one of the cups of

56

what appeared to be tea. "He is…unkind to me."

She received it and took a brief sip. She frowned at his words. "Oh. I'm sorry."

He shrugged. "It is what it is. How about you? Are you and your *schweschder* friends?"

"We get along fine, but I wouldn't say we're particularly close. She's quite a bit older. Eight years. She doesn't attend the youth gatherings anymore."

"How old are you, then?" They each sat down on one of the folding chairs set up on the lawn next to the barn. Jacob was pleased with their easy conversation.

She ducked her head. "*Ach*, I'm just barely sixteen."

Jah, she was young. But not too young. He could be patient if he had to. What was a couple of years?

"How old are you?"

"Twenty-three."

"Seven years older than me."

"*Jah*." He shifted to study her. "Is there someone I should talk to about asking to take you home? I mean, if I'm not too old for your liking."

Her cheeks darkened and she lowered her lashes. "*Nee*. And I…I don't think you're too *alt*."

"How do you think your father would feel? Would he approve?"

She shrugged. "I think he maybe would. He might like to meet you."

"Where do you live?"

"Down the road from the schoolhouse. *Mei schweschder* teaches there. Has since she was my age."

"She is not married?"

"*Nee.*" Rachel shrugged. "Sometimes she is sick. I think her condition scares off potential *ehemann.*"

"Oh. I'm sorry." He didn't really know what to say about her sister, but he felt bad for her nonetheless. It wondered him if this was the 'Leah' Jeriah had spoken of. "Is she expected to get better?"

"*Nee,* she'll only get worse. But she's not too bad yet. Most people don't even know. *Dat* didn't really want us telling people because he didn't want to scare off *buwe,* but several people know. It's hard to keep secrets in the *g'may.*"

"I won't say anything to anybody."

"I don't really think it's that big of a deal. *Dat* was just hoping she'd be able to find some happiness. Marriage and *kinner* bring lots of joy into your life."

"*Jah,* they usually do."

"But no man wants to marry a *fraa* that isn't expected to survive long. I mean, if she did marry and have *kinner* and then she passed, who would raise the *kinner*? Her *ehemann* would have to work to provide."

"*Ach,* I see the problem."

Jacob thought of his twin brother. Maybe Leah

would have been a suitable mate for Ephraim, had he not been interested in that *Englisch* girl. He quickly dismissed the thought. In his current state, or at least when Jacob had left home, Ephraim had wanted to kill him. He likely would not be doing him favors anytime soon or listening to his advice on anything, let alone *maed*. Besides, Ephraim and his *Englisch maed* had been dating long enough now that they could very likely be planning to get hitched. *Mamm* had mentioned their fear of him marrying the *maedel*.

"She's never really talked about it, at least not to me. I don't think she minds one way or another."

"Are you sure and certain about that? I mean, if she's a school teacher, she's obviously fond of *kinner*. Ain't so?" Jacob's heart went out to Rachel's poor sister. It must be a terrible predicament for an Amish woman.

She shrugged. "I don't know. I reckon."

He noticed the volleyball game winding down. "When will the singing start?"

"Should be any minute now."

"Do you already have a ride home then, for afterwards?" *Please let her say no, Gott.*

"I do."

His heart sank to his feet, till he caught the sparkle in her eye.

"At least, I *think* I do. Unless you've changed your mind."

A winning bet on the horse racing track that some of his father's clients attended could not have made him change his mind. Not that he would ever bet.

"*Nee*, I haven't changed my mind." He grinned.

NINE

Rachel leaned forward in the buggy when they pulled into her driveway. It was apparent there were still a couple of lanterns lit, which meant *Dat* was probably still awake. Should she bring Jacob inside even if *Dat* was still up?

Spending an evening with Jacob had almost been like a dream, and she didn't want it to end. Aside from the butterflies flitting around in her tummy, she'd felt completely at ease with Jacob King.

"*Ach*, it looks like *mei vatter* is awake." She chewed on her bottom lip.

"Would this be a *gut* time to meet him?" His expression was eager.

"I think it might be okay."

He reached over and grasped her hand for the third time that evening. Each time, she'd welcomed it. "I had a *gut* time with you, Rachel. But just in case I don't get a chance to say a proper goodbye later, is it all right if I say it now?"

Her face heated. What did he mean by his words? Did he mean…?

Her eyes widened as he moved close and briefly brushed her lips with his. Her heartbeat raced and her eyes instinctively draped shut, but the moment ended all too soon. *Ach*, his lips had been soft and his kiss had been wonderful gentle. It was better than what she'd imagined a first kiss would be like, but, *ach*, she wanted to do it again. Longer.

"Was that okay?" he murmured.

"*Nee*." She really needed another taste of his peppermint kisses.

He moved back and studied her. "*Nee*? I'm sorry, I should have waited till—"

"It wasn't long enough." Her words tumbled out. She ignored propriety and pulled Jacob close.

"*Ach*…" Instead of saying another word, he cupped her cheek with his warm hand and brought his lips down on hers once again. This time, he kissed with intention, as though he were a thirsty man in a desert and her lips were the only water that could quench him.

She tilted her head as his lips seemed to explore hers. She followed wherever he was leading, craving his woodsy cologne and minty breath more with every second that passed. She had no idea how this was supposed to go and wondered if he thought she did.

No wonder why her friend Judy liked kissing *buwe* so much! *Now* she understood. Jacob was…*ach*, he was like a dream…a fantasy.

He finally broke away when a slight noise sounded from inside the house. *Jah*, *Dat* was still up. Hopefully, he or Leah hadn't been watching from behind the curtain.

Jacob's breathing was ragged. "Mm…that was…nice. Very nice."

"*Jah*, I liked it too."

"*Gut*. I didn't know if I was doing it right."

"It was…" She couldn't help her breathy voice. "It was *your* first time too?"

"*Jah*. You are the first girl I've ever really been interested in."

Her heart sang. *Ach*, he'd saved up that kiss just for her? She felt like a queen. Was Jacob the one? She already knew she could gaze into those brooding eyes every day of her life, for sure and certain. But it was way too soon to be making any lifelong plans just yet, wasn't it? *Jah*, she was getting ahead of herself.

He glanced back toward the house. "Should we go inside?"

"Are you…are you done saying goodbye?" Warmth

spread through Rachel's entire being. She couldn't believe her boldness. *Ach*, she felt like she could sit out in the buggy with Jacob all night.

He traced her lips with his thumb, a look of longing in his eyes. "I don't know if I'll ever be done."

He cleared his throat. "But your *vatter* might get suspicious if we're sitting out in my buggy kissing all night. I don't want him to get the wrong idea. I wouldn't want him to think I'd dishonor you."

"*Dat*, this is Jacob King. He is new to our community." Rachel tried not to appear too eager in front of her father. She turned to Jacob. "This is *mei vatter*, Marlin. He is also the deacon of our *g'may*."

Jacob stretched his hand toward her father. "*Gut* to meet you."

Marlin shook Jacob's hand and nodded. Rachel caught the twinkle in her father's eye. He rubbed his hands together. "Tell me about yourself, Jacob."

Ach, they seemed to be getting along. This was a *gut* sign.

She smiled as she moved to the kitchen to prepare a snack and coffee for the three of them. Should she prepare an extra cup in case Leah joined them downstairs? *Jah*, she would. She'd never want Jacob to think she was inconsiderate.

A few moments later, she reentered the living room. Jacob and her father were deep in conversation. She attempted to listen.

"I'm sure it is difficult keeping up with your property, having the burdens of a deacon." Jacob said. "You only have two *maed*? No sons?"

"*Ach, jah. Der Herr* never saw fit to give *mei fraa* and me *sohns*. But we're thankful for our *dochdern*. It seems I am always falling behind on everything, though."

Rachel offered each of them a steaming cup of coffee along with one of the muffins she and Leah had made yesterday. She set the tray down on the table, then joined the two men.

"*Denki, Rachel.*" Jacob's sincere smile took her breath away.

She nodded demurely.

He took a sip of his coffee, then looked to her father. "I'm working at the flooring shop right now full time during the day, but I'd be happy to come over and help you out after I'm finished for the day."

Ach, Jacob was kind and thoughtful and hardworking. A man Rachel could easily admire.

"You would do that?"

"Sure, I'd be happy to. Besides, it would give me a chance to get to know your *dochder* better."

He glanced up and boldly shot Rachel a wink. *Ach*, what must her *vatter* think of this forward man?

Dat's face became animated. *Ach*, he must have really taken a liking to Jacob. "That would be *wunderbaar*. And you could take supper with us."

"I'd like that. I can start tomorrow." He scratched the stubble on his chin. "We should have a few hours for working, especially in summer yet."

She'd get to see Jacob and have supper with him every day? *Ach*, that almost sounded too *gut* to be true!

"I…I won't be able to pay you." Her father frowned.

"I wasn't expecting anything. It will be my pleasure. My *vatter* owns a large horse ranch in Kentucky. I enjoy caring for the animals. I can do most anything required on a ranch. Just put me to work."

"*Wunderbaar*, Jacob. *Der Herr* has sent you our way, I'm sure of it." *Dat* beamed.

Jacob's gaze moved to Rachel. His eyes studied her intently. *Ach*, was he remembering their kisses in the buggy too?

Dat nodded, eyeing the two of them. He knew they were sweet on each other for sure and for certain.

TEN

er Herr had been smiling down on him and Jacob knew it. *Ach*, it seemed He was leading him every step of the way, holding his hand in this new community.

Wasn't that why he'd gotten along so well with his host family and others in the *g'may*? Wasn't that why he'd secured a job so quickly—a job he enjoyed?

And of course he'd met Rachel. Wonderful Rachel. He knew it was still early in their relationship, but as far as he could see, she was everything he'd always dreamed of in a *maedel*. In a *fraa*. *Mamm* and *Dat* had been wise in sending him to this community.

He'd enjoyed working side-by-side with Marlin. The man really seemed to have taken a liking to him. Perhaps he was glad to see someone interested in one of his *dochdern*. That was quite possible, considering that his oldest *dochder* had been deemed an *alt maedel* in their community.

Jacob followed Marlin's leading into the house, first washing up at the mudroom sink. *Ach*, he wished he could take a shower too, before seeing Rachel. She'd likely want a kiss goodnight—he knew he did—and he wanted to smell *gut* for her. But he hadn't even the forethought to bring along an extra set of clothes. *Au naturel* is how he would have to remain. Oh well, she was likely used to the primal scent of a hardworking man. A trait common in their culture.

"Jacob, this is my oldest *dochder*, Leah." Marlin moved close to the woman at the sink and lightly kissed her cheek.

Jah, he loved his *dochdern*.

"*Gut* to meet you, Leah." Jacob grinned at the homely blonde. She seemed thin, to his thinking. Was that part of the sickness Rachel had mentioned? His heart went out to Leah.

He couldn't see any reason the *buwe* in this community wouldn't have courted her. She wasn't as *schee* as his Rachel, but she certainly wasn't ugly.

She nodded demurely. "Welcome to our home."

"*Denki*." He glanced around the room, but didn't see Rachel.

"She'll be down soon, Jacob. Likely wants to look her best for her beau." Marlin chuckled.

Ach, so Marlin suspected they were courting. *Gut*.

Because he had every intention not only to court Rachel Schmidt, but to marry her someday too, *Gott* willing.

"Is there anything I can help out with?" He offered.

"*Nee*," Leah said. "As soon as Rachel comes downstairs, we can sit down to eat. Everything is pretty much ready."

Marlin eyed Jacob. "Why don't you go fetch her?"

"You want *me* to go...upstairs?" Jacob's jaw slacked. Surely he'd thought that would be considered inappropriate. But if he had Rachel's *vatter's* permission...

Marlin nodded.

Jacob didn't need any more encouragement. He considered finding Rachel a privilege. As soon as he hit the top of the stairs, he listened for movement.

Rachel's bedroom must be to the right of the hallway. But he shouldn't just walk in. What if she was...

He cleared his throat. "Uh, Rachel?" He squeaked out.

"*Ach*!" He heard her gasp before he saw her. "Jacob?" She poked her head out of a room.

She was gorgeous as ever. A million years could pass and he'd never tire of beholding her beautiful countenance. And her smile. *Ach*. Just her smile seemed to make his knees weak.

"Your *dat* said I could find you up here." He glanced

back toward the stairs. "Leah said supper is ready."

He was unsure how their household was run, but he guessed tonight was Leah's night to make supper. He'd ask Rachel later. Right now, he just wanted to claim a kiss before they had to rush downstairs.

"Okay." She eyed him timidly and stepped out of her room.

He inched near, begging permission with his gaze. At her consensual nod, he pulled her into his arms and dipped his head. His lips brushed hers, reminding him how *gut* a kiss with Rachel felt. Hopefully she felt the same way about him. Her arms wrapped around him, but he stepped back.

"*Ach*, I'm sorry. I've been outside working. I know I can't smell *gut*. And I'm likely all sweaty."

She opened her mouth to speak. "I—"

"You two coming or should we eat without you?" Marlin's voice called up the stairs.

"Uh, *jah*, we're coming," Rachel hollered, her cheeks rosy. She took a deep breath and tugged on his hand, leading the way to the stairs. "*Kumm*."

If Jacob had his way, he'd tell Marlin and Leah to go ahead and eat without them. If only…

They could eat anytime. Kisses were few and far between. Then again, if they stayed upstairs…alone… kissing. *Nee*, that would *not* be a wise idea.

He didn't know how Rachel did it, but she held this unseen power over him. He was clay in her hands and she could mold him into anything, talk him into anything, get him to do anything.

How in *der welt* was that possible? They'd only met just yesterday.

Ach, she was dangerous. A wild exciting crazy dangerous. And, *Gott* help him, he loved her. Craved her. Needed her.

Jah, kissing alone in a bedroom would definitely have to wait till *after* they were married. Because he was sure and certain that she was, without a doubt, *the one*.

ELEVEN

After supper, Jacob insisted on helping Rachel with the dishes. *Dat* sat in his usual place in the living room—his beloved hickory rocker that matched *Mamm's*—and read *The Budget* newspaper. Leah had retreated to her room again. It seemed she'd been spending more and more time there. Alone.

Rachel's heart ached for her *schweschder*. What must it be like to walk in her shoes? What was *Der Herr's* plan for her life? Surely not pain and suffering. Surely not a life alone. But who was she to guess at what *Gott's* purposes were for another person? *Nee*, she couldn't even begin to think she knew the thoughts of *Der Herr*.

A sudden verse she'd heard during church popped into her head. *For I know the thoughts I think toward you, saith the LORD. Thoughts of good and not of evil. To give you an expected end.*

Jah, Der Herr desired *gut*. Even for Leah. But how? When?

With dishes now finished, Jacob grasped her hand and tugged her toward the door.

"Just a minute." She held up a finger, then stuck her head around the wall into the living room. "*Dat*, Jacob and I are going out."

"I won't wait up for you," *Dat* called.

Gut. Because if there was a chill in the air, she'd like the option of ducking into the house, with privacy.

They stepped outside and Jacob pointed to one of the fields. "I saw your sheep today."

Her smile widened. She loved caring for her sheep. They were friendly, yet docile, and they followed her as soon as she came near. Sometimes, she didn't even need to speak a word.

"Do you use their wool?"

She nodded. "I process it and sell it. *Kumm*, I will show you."

Excitement spiraled in her belly at the thought of showing Jacob a huge part of her world. Hopefully, he'd love it just as much as she did.

They stepped into the barn and she led him to her wool production wing. Too bad it was the wrong time of year for processing so he wouldn't be able to see the production in action.

"Wow! This looks impressive. What is it?" He chuckled.

"Well, first of all, *Dat* and I bring the sheep in and keep them in this large stall. They tend to like to stay together and it's less distressing to them." She explained. "Then, one by one, we bring them out and shear them."

She showed him the shears.

"Electric?"

"*Jah*. We have a generator that powers our electric equipment. We separate the wool, depending on which part of the body it's from.

"After that, we put it into this and fill it with very hot water." She pointed to their giant cast iron pot that had always reminded her of a witch's cauldron she'd seen in a Halloween display. "Then we leave it for a day."

"Why?"

"It separates the lanolin. Lanolin is like an oil in the fiber that can be used for creams and lotions. So, after it's been sitting, the next day, we collect the lanolin. It rises to the top of the water and we just skim it off."

He nodded. "Interesting."

"*Jah*. Sheep are such useful creatures." She smiled. "From there, we wash the fleece. It takes a couple of rinses to get it nice and white. We put it out on screens to dry. Then after it dries, we pull it apart to thin it out. We try to remove the pieces of grass and debris."

She picked up a pair of flat brushes. "After that, we card it. It's basically similar to brushing hair." She pointed to their carding machine. It was a contraption that had two thick wooden dowel-like wheels. One was fat and the other was much smaller. They both had tiny metal spikes like the brushes. It was turned by a handle on the side.

"What is that?"

"You can either card it by hand or use this. This is a carding machine. We run the wool through it and it thins it out and makes it kind of fluffy." She demonstrated by turning the handle.

"From there, we pull it into long strips called roving, then I will take the roving, pull them to a certain thickness and put a little twist into it, then feed them through this." She pointed to a wooden spinning wheel. "This will spin and collect the yarn on the bobbin. It's pretty much done after that."

"Do you sell it then?"

She nodded. "*Jah*. I will take it to the dry goods store and they sell it for me."

"You are a remarkable woman, Rachel King." He pulled her close and into his arms. The look of admiration in his eyes was unmistakable.

She gasped when she realized what he'd said. She leaned back and stared at him, searching his eyes. Surely he was teasing. "*King*?"

"I can dream, can't I?"

"*Jah*, but I don't think the leaders are going to approve of a marriage after two days." She smiled, content to be in Jacob's strong arms, hearing his heart beat against her ear. *Ach*, she could stay like this forever.

"I know. We'll have to be patient, for sure. I'm just staking my claim." He caught her eye and winked, then brushed her lips with a soft kiss.

"I'm all yours," she whispered.

"*Nee*, not yet."

"My heart is, I mean."

"I'm glad to hear it. I think you know where my heart lies." The back of his hand slowly trailed her cheek.

Jah, next to mine. What would it be to lie next to Jacob as his *fraa*? Her cheeks warmed at the thought. "I think I love you." *Ach*, had she really said that out loud? Oh, no. "*Ach*, I mean—"

He put a finger to her lips. "Shh…"

He gazed into her eyes. "I *know* I love you. I don't know how, but somehow, before we even talked to each other, it's like my heart said '*that is her.*' It seems like

77

sometimes, the heart just knows."

"Maybe it was *Der Herr*."

"*Ach*, it was definitely *Der Herr*. I have no doubt about that." He stepped back. "Rachel, before we…I…I need to tell you something."

"You can share anything with me."

He shook his head. "You won't want to hear this. It is not *gut*."

He moved away from her touch, leaving her bereft.

She wished she could wipe the frown and the look of worry from his face.

"But you should know. Especially if you are to become my *fraa* someday."

"Should…" She swallowed. "Should I be worried?"

He shrugged, his eyes pained. "Maybe."

"What is it, Jacob?"

"It's about why I left home." He paced the barn floor. "I was selfish, Rachel. I was wrong. I'm ashamed to even admit what I did."

Worry took root in Rachel's heart. *Please, Gott. I don't want to lose Jacob. Whatever it is, give me understanding. Help us through it.*

"What did you do?" Her voice emerged feathery and whispered.

"I stole something. Well, not quite stole. I tricked my brother into signing over *mei vatter's* property to me. And I deceived *mei vatter* by changing Ephraim's name to my own without *Dat's* permission." He blew out a breath. "But now *Dat* won't change the will back. He says it is *Der Herr's* will. And my brother, Ephraim, he wants to kill me."

"What?"

"It is why my *mamm* and *dat* sent me here. Well, for that reason and to find a *fraa*. I didn't lie about that part."

"So, money is important to you then? More important than relationships?" The thought hurt her heart. But the Bible did say that the love of money is the root of all evil. She didn't want to think of Jacob as evil, though.

"*Nee*, not at all."

"Well, then, why?"

"I've always craved *mei vatter's* approval, but he's always favored *mei bruder,* Ephraim. I thought that, well, somehow this would change things. Ephraim isn't a *gut* man. He's always been rebellious, yet *Dat* has continuously supported him. I never understood that." Emotion pricked Jacob's voice and she longed to comfort him.

Ach, he was like a little child inside. He was hurting. Doing anything and everything just to get his *vatter* to notice him, to no avail.

"But forcing someone to love you when they don't…" He broke down in tears.

Rachel stepped near and gathered him into her arms. "*Ach*, Jacob. I'm sure your *vatter* loves you in his own way."

She wished she could write a letter to Jacob's father letting him know the immense grief his son suffered. She was certain that they'd never sat down and had a heart-to-heart conversation. Sometimes, things could be resolved, or at least better understood, if the two parties came together for a heartfelt discussion.

She knew it wasn't her place, but she was determined to do it anyway. Jacob's father *needed* to know how his son felt.

"And your *mamm*?" she asked.

"*Ach*, I've never doubted *Mamm's* love. She has always supported me. She was my best friend."

"I'm glad to hear that."

He took in a deep breath and pulled away. "I'm sorry."

"Don't be. You are a human being with human emotions. They are given to us by *Der Herr*. Never feel ashamed of them." She pulled him back into her arms.

"You are not disappointed?" He mumbled into her head scarf.

"*Nee*. I am not perfect, either. I have sinned too."

80

She pulled back now and stared at him. "Were you required to make a kneeling confession?"

"*Nee*. They let *Dat* and I work it out since it was a family matter. And since *Dat* had chalked it up to *Gott's* will…" He shrugged. "But I have since confessed to *Der Herr*."

"That is what matters, ain't so?"

"*Jah*." He nodded. "But someday, if *mei bruder* ever gets over his anger, I need to apologize to him too. Even if he was wrong on his part too."

She didn't know exactly what his brother's part was, but she trusted Jacob to expound if he thought it was necessary. Better to let him share in his own time.

"You are a *gut* man, Jacob King." She studied him in admiration.

"How can you say that? I just told you that I was greedy and deceitful and—"

"And the man I'd be honored to call *mei ehemann*."

He traced her cheek with his finger. "*Ach*, Rachel. I am not worthy of you. For sure, it was *Der Herr* who brought me here. I have no doubt of that now."

Rachel closed her eyes as he bent toward her. Kissing Jacob felt like the most right thing in the world at this moment. Nothing was going to separate them, she was sure of it. She would be Jacob's for always and forever.

TWELVE

Nine months later…

*J*acob's heart somersaulted as Marlin stood up to speak to the congregation. In their district, it was the deacon's job to publish engaged couples' intentions to marry—a ceremony that would typically commence within the following month or two.

"Now, I will announce the *banns*." Marlin suppressed what looked like a mischievous smile.

Jacob's own grin stretched from ear-to-ear. He couldn't help it. *Ach*, this was one of the most exciting days of his life!

"Jacob King and Leah Schmidt will marry on Tuesday of the following week at our farm."

Jacob's cheeks warmed and his head snapped up to look at Marlin.

Leah? *Nee*, her father had misspoken. He'd surely meant to say Rachel's name. He wouldn't correct him

83

in front of the entire congregation, though. That was not his place.

Jacob's eyes roamed the *g'may* and found his intended, shooting a wink in her direction. They both rose from their seats and immediately left the *haus*.

Jacob reached for Rachel's hand as soon as they were out of view of the congregation. He'd almost pulled her into his arms, when they spotted Leah coming up behind them.

"Why are you coming along, *schweschder*?" Rachel twisted and dropped Jacob's hand, to his disappointment.

"*Ach, Dat* urged me to leave too."

"But why?" Rachel frowned. "This is mine and Jacob's time to be together. Alone."

Leah shrugged. "*Dat* insisted. I don't know why. Would you have me disobey him?"

"*Ach, nee.* Of course, not."

Jacob sensed Rachel's frustration and felt a little himself. Why *had* their father sent Leah along? It was not the way things were typically done. Hopefully, he and Rachel could still find some alone time. He was looking forward to sharing a few private kisses with his beloved.

Rachel had prepared a romantic meal for two in advance, and the two of them took their picnic lunch down to the pond. Leah stayed up at the house, although Jacob was certain Marlin had sent her along as a chaperone. But they didn't need or want a chaperone. Okay, maybe they *should* have had one present to restrain their kisses, but they were to be wed in just over a week. He hadn't dishonored this betrothed, but they'd probably crossed the lines of propriety for an unmarried couple...*jah*, maybe a chaperone wouldn't have been a bad idea.

Ach, he couldn't wait to make Rachel his *fraa*. It was a *gut* thing their wedding would take place in just over a week. He couldn't imagine waiting much longer than that.

Marlin joined the family at home after the common meal had ended. Now, he and Jacob sat in the living area. The *maed* had disappeared into the kitchen to give them time to talk.

"Did you realize that you misspoke when you read the *banns*? You said Leah's name instead of Rachel." Jacob expelled an easy chuckle.

"*Nee*, I did not misspeak."

"You said Leah."

"Perhaps, but I did not speak the wrong name."

Jacob frowned and stared at Marlin. His declaration

85

confused him. "It is *Rachel* I will marry."

"*Nee*, you will marry my Leah." He insisted.

"I'm not marrying Leah."

"Then you will not marry my Rachel."

What? His gaze shot to Rachel, who prepared snacks in the kitchen, then to Leah helping her. Did either of them know anything about their father's ludicrous statement?

"But, I thought you said I could marry your *dochder*. I meant Rachel when I'd asked you, not Leah. You know very well I've been courting Rachel the past nine months. I have no interest in Leah."

"Leah is older. She must marry first."

"Out of all due respect, I do not think you are thinking straight."

"Leah will marry first. There is no other man old enough to marry her and I do not want her to become an *alt maedel*."

"Perhaps there is a man in another district who will marry your oldest *dochder*? Or a widower?"

"*Nee*, there is no one. Only you." He leaned close and whispered to Jacob. "She is sickly. She likely will not be around long anyhow."

"But I…I'm planning to marry Rachel." He repeated.

"Leah must raise *grossbopplin*. You must not deny her this."

"I'm not denying Leah anything. I'm in love with *Rachel*. *She* is the one I will marry on Tuesday." Anger clenched his fists.

Marlin stared him in the eye. His resolve firm. "You will *never* be allowed to marry Rachel or see her again, if you do not agree to this thing."

"I won't be allowed to see Rach… You cannot force me to marry Leah! It is wrong."

"Maybe so. But the choice is yours."

"This is not a choice!" He cried in frustration. "This is foolishness."

"If that is the way you feel, then we have nothing more to speak to each other about. You may leave my property and this community and go back to where you came from. Do not come back seeking *mei dochder's* hand. Ever."

Jacob's throat tightened. Was he going to suffocate? This could not be happening. One cannot just change the bride days before the wedding. Who had ever heard of such a thing?

Ach, he had to do something. "And if I take Rachel with me?"

"You do not want to play that game with me, Jacob. Rachel is still under age. I will have you arrested for kidnapping."

Ach, who was the one playing games? Arrested? Was he serious? He'd never be able to see Rachel again? He couldn't bear the thought.

He glanced her way, then looked to Leah. The two seemed to be lost in conversation. Rachel beamed like a young woman who was about to be married. It seemed neither of them were privy to their *vatter's* shenanigans.

Perhaps he could leave, then talk Rachel into meeting him as soon as she was of age. They could move away and marry elsewhere.

Marlin nodded curtly, dismissing him. "Fine. I will marry Rachel off to someone else then." Marlin stood, as though that was his final word.

"You can't do that!" Could he?

"Watch me."

Ach, what on earth was he going to do?

"You may leave now," Marlin insisted.

"But I…" He had no idea what to say or do to make this right. He didn't want to lose Rachel, which was what would surely happen if he left. "Let me talk to Rachel. Please."

"Very well. Come back tomorrow after you've had time to think this through."

A plan took form in his mind. Surely, the leaders would not approve of this scheme of Marlin's. He would meet with the leaders tonight, then approach Rachel with his *gut* news in the morning. Whatever he did, he needed to hurry. Time was *not* on his side.

THIRTEEN

*J*acob stood on the Schmidt family's porch and knocked on the door. His heart beat a million times per minute, it seemed. He wasn't looking forward to this conversation. *Nee*, he was dreading it.

His beautiful bride-to-be stood in the doorway. *Nee*, not bride-to-be.

"Rachel…" Jacob's voice sounded breathless to his own ears. "*Kumm*, we need to talk."

"Are…are you okay?" He heard the distress in her voice, no doubt a reaction to his bleary eyes. He'd tossed and turned all night long praying for a solution.

She must've recognized the seriousness in his tone and took his proffered hand, allowing him to lead them outside. They sat down on the porch swing.

"I don't know how to say this, Rachel." He stood and began pacing.

"Say what?" She shivered.

Ach, but how *could* he say this? He looked away from her. He did not want to see the hurt in her eyes.

"Please, Jacob. I've never seen you like this. You're scaring me."

"I…your father…I can't marry you."

"You can't…?" She shook her head. "What *about* my father? What did he say to you?" She frowned, sounding more angry than hurt.

"You won't like this. I don't like it." He practically drew blood as he bit the inside of his cheek. "I don't want to hurt you. *Ach*, you're the last person in the world I'd want to hurt. I'm sorry, *lieb*. So sorry." He couldn't help it when moisture surfaced in his eyes.

"What?" Her voice shook. Dread likely filled her heart as it had his.

He squeezed his eyes shut, willing this nightmare to cease. But it wouldn't. "Your father is insisting that I marry your *schweschder*."

"*Leah*? Why?"

Why indeed? He shrugged. "He says she must marry first."

"He can't do that!" Tears sprung to Rachel's eyes the moment he'd said the words. *Ach*, he knew she'd be upset. *He* was upset. But he didn't know what he could do about it.

He'd already gone to the other leaders in the district

and stated his case. They'd unanimously sided with Marlin. He was the patriarch, the girls' *dat* and leader of the home, and he had final say in whom they married. If he was against a particular union, they were convinced he had good reason, and they would honor his wishes. No doubt his deacon status held clout in their community as well. They would not interfere in the matter.

"Apparently, he can. I've already approached the other leaders. They sided with your father."

Jacob didn't understand. Something like this would never happen in his district back in Kentucky. Shouldn't it be each person's choice whom they marry? He wished to marry Rachel. Rachel wanted to marry him. It wasn't complicated. If only he and Rachel had met in his district. But they hadn't.

"Why would he do this?" He heard the desperation in her voice.

"I don't think he means it to slight you. He just wants Leah to have a family of her own. For some reason, he's chosen *me* as the one to make that a reality."

"But you told him you love *me*, right? You told him that you want to marry *me*, not Leah."

"*Jah*, I did. He will not listen to me, *schatzi*. He doesn't care about you or me or our love for each other."

"But you will not agree to it, ain't so?"

"I don't want to, but…" *Ach*, this was the most difficult thing he'd ever faced.

"But what?" She shook her head. "You're actually considering it?"

"What choice do I have, Rachel? If I do not marry your sister, I must leave. Your father insisted that if I do not marry Leah, he would give you away to someone else. I cannot bear the thought of that."

"This doesn't make any sense."

"His idea is that I will marry your sister, then marry you when she passes. Since she is sickly, he figures it won't be too long." He clenched his fists. "*Ach*, I hate the thought of this whole scheme. It's not fair to you, me, or Leah."

"So you would marry her and then we'd just wait for her to die?"

"It's terrible, I know." He smashed his lips together. "Your father wants her to have *kinner* and raise a family in the time she has left."

"You…you would share the marriage bed with *mei schweschder*?" Her bottom lip trembled and a flow of tears ensued.

He turned away. "I'm sorry, Rachel. If there was another way…"

"I can't believe you're considering this."

"What else can we do? Your father promised me that he would save you for me if I agree to do this. I'm afraid it is the only way we can marry."

"*Jah*, but when? Who knows how long my sister will live? I could be past my time to have *bopplin* by the time we marry."

"Your father said the doctor gave her five years to live. Can we wait five years?"

She wiped away her tears and fastened her arms across her chest. She shook her head. "I don't know."

He moved close and lifted her chin with his forefinger. She looked away. "Look at me, Rachel." He waited until she did. He gazed into her forlorn eyes. *Ach*, how he hated causing her grief. "My love for you will never ever die. I do not love your sister. I do not *desire* to marry your sister. I want to marry you."

"I want to marry you too."

He bent down and pressed his lips to hers. *Ach*, he desperately needed her. He didn't know how he'd be able to live without her. He crushed her to his chest, and wrapped his arms around her, never wanting to let her go.

"If I could, I'd whisk you away this instant and marry you. But I cannot do that. You are not yet of age." He frowned into her kerchief. He'd consider moving back home with her, but not if his brother still sought to kill him. "But then we'd have to leave our people and live as the *Englisch*."

"Or be put in the *bann*."

"Whatever is decided, we must be in agreement. The only reason I'd ever even consider marrying your *schweschder* is so that I could marry you. If I wasn't promised a future with you, I'd leave altogether. Because I couldn't bear the thought of seeing you married to another man."

"Yet, you will be marrying another woman."

"Do I have a choice?" Could she hear the anguish in his voice? This was not his will at all.

"*Ach*, I suppose not."

"Rachel, I will do anything you want. I would do anything for you. I love you so much, my heart cries for you."

"I know you do."

"Let's pray about this. Perhaps *Der Herr* will show us another way."

"*Jah*, we can do that. For sure and certain."

FOURTEEN

Rachel reluctantly approached her father after Leah had gone upstairs to her room. He sat in his usual spot, reading *The Budget* newspaper. As though all was well in his world. As though her world were not crumbling around her.

She approached and sat in the hickory rocker nearest him. Perhaps she could talk some sense into him. If he just saw how upsetting this whole situation was, maybe he'd change his mind.

He glanced over the newspaper. His probing gaze met hers through his spectacles. "Did you wish to say something, *dochder*?"

She stared down at her hands. "*Jah*, I...I talked to Jacob." *Ach*, she'd told herself she wouldn't cry.

"And has he agreed to my plan?"

She shook her head. "Why? Why are you doing this? You know I love Jacob and Jacob loves me."

He folded the paper onto his lap. "This is best, *dochder*."

"Best?" Her voice screeched. "Best for who? For you?"

"*Nee*. For everyone."

"How can you believe that? You know that is not true."

"It is true, *dochder*." Her father didn't actually believe his own words, did he? How could he?

"Help me make sense of this, *Dat*. Why would you want to give the man I love to my sister?"

"She is older. She needs to marry first."

Indignation rose in her throat, but she forced the words down. She wouldn't get anywhere by disrespecting her father. "Why? And why my Jacob?"

"He is but two years younger than Leah. All of the other *bu* are much younger. And I have already approached several of them."

That didn't explain anything.

"You are only sixteen yet. You have plenty of years ahead of you. Your sister will likely only have a few more."

Jah, she felt terrible for her sister, but not enough to give up her own future for her. Leah's illness was indeed a tragedy. But it wasn't Jacob's or her fault that her sister was sick. "It is not fair to force Jacob to marry Leah."

96

"I am not forcing him. It is his choice."

"But you said you wouldn't allow him to marry me if he didn't first marry Leah. To me, that is forcing."

"Will you deny Leah the one chance to have a family of her own?"

"It is not of her own if it is with Jacob. He belongs to me."

He sighed. "I will tell you the whole truth now, *dochder*. Perhaps you will be able to understand then."

The *whole* truth? What did he mean? She frowned, but waited for her father to continue.

"When you were very young, just a little more than a *boppli* yet, you were in an accident. That accident caused injuries to your body. The *dochter* said you would not be able to have *bopplin*."

She gasped. *Nee*, that couldn't be true!

Tears welled in her eyes. Were her father's words sincere? She'd be childless? Her heart squeezed so tight she didn't think she'd be able to breathe. How could she marry Jacob if she couldn't give him *bopplin*? *Jah*, he'd probably agree to marry her anyway, but it wouldn't be fair to him. What Amish man did not want *kinner* of his own? Usually a houseful.

"So you see? If Jacob marries Leah, they will be doing you a favor. They will have the *bopplin*, your *schweschder* will get to have a family, and then when your *schweschder* is no longer with us, Jacob can marry you and you will have *kinner* to raise."

Rachel sat numb. She hated that her father's idea somewhat made sense. "Does...does Jacob know that I cannot have *bopplin*?"

"I have not mentioned it. I thought it would be better for you if he did not know." He placed his hand over hers, a gesture of affection not typically seen in her home. "I know this is difficult *dochder*, but I believe it is best for all involved."

She shook her head, denying his words. "*Nee*, it is not."

Her father frowned. "Don't get any foolish notions about sneaking off with that *bu*, either. I'm sure he is likely to try to talk you into it."

"What if I did run away with Jacob? You wouldn't be able to stop us," she said defiantly.

Fire sparked in his eyes. "You do *not* want to do that, *dochder*."

"But I do. Don't you understand? I want to marry Jacob more than anything, *Dat*."

"More than seeing your beloved Jacob in prison? Because, I assure you, *dochder*, if he attempts to run off with you, that is where he will be. In prison for kidnapping. And you will never be allowed to marry him." He frowned. "Is that what you want?"

"You know it isn't."

"Trust me, *dochder*. I know what is best."

"*Nee*, you don't! You don't know anything." She sprung from her chair and sprinted up the stairs to her room, then slammed the door for effect. She buried her head into her pillow and cried until she thought her tears would run dry.

"Why, *Gott*? Why? It isn't fair."

FIFTEEN

"My *vatter* is not going to change his mind, Jacob." Rachel shoved away a tear. "I tried talking to him. He is like a stone wall."

He thrust his hands into his pockets and frowned. "Will you...would you consider coming away with me? We could leave tonight."

"You...you would want to leave? Just the two of us?" Her eyes grew wide. "Where would we go? We could not marry yet."

"*Nee*, not until you're of age."

"But my father said that he would call the police. He warned me you'd want to do this. He is serious, Jacob. I do not doubt that he would have you arrested."

"*Ach*, I did not think he was serious. That is not the way of our people."

"He meant it, Jacob, for sure and certain."

"I'm willing to risk being arrested for you."

"Prison would be worse than marrying *mei schweschder*, ain't so? There are really bad men in those prisons. At least you'd be safe here. And you'd likely be in prison longer than Leah will be alive. Besides, you could not be Amish in jail. They would turn you into an *Englischer* and you would learn the ways of the world."

He sighed, no doubt relinquishing the idea as she had.

She bowed her head. "Jacob, I…I need to tell you something."

"What? What is it?" He must've sensed her seriousness.

"My father told me something I never knew." She inhaled deeply, willing her tears to stay hidden. She'd already cried so much and she was exhausted. But she couldn't help it. Sometimes she wished she could be one of those people who didn't let anything faze them. But that wasn't her. She couldn't deny that the pain of this situation ran deep. She couldn't imagine it away even if she wanted to. "I was in an accident at a very young age. The doctors made surgery. Jacob, I…I cannot have *kinner*."

"What?" His mouth fell open. She read the disappointment in his eyes and she hated it.

"I'm sorry." Rachel shrugged. "So you see, maybe

it's best that you marry *mei schweschder*." She barely squeaked the words out before the dam broke.

Jacob pulled her into his arms and smoothed her hair at the nape of her neck. "Shh…*ach*, it's okay, Rachel. You should know by now that nothing can make me love you less. Do you hear me?"

"*Jah*, I hear you. But it is not easy to believe."

"*Ach*, your worth is not based on whether you are able to have *kinner* or not. *My love* is not based on whether you are able to have *kinner* or not." He leaned down and pressed his lips to hers, as if to prove his point.

How much longer would they be able to do this? Part of Rachel just wanted to throw caution to the wind. What would happen if Jacob did dishonor her? Would the two of them be forced to marry? Maybe if…

She pressed close and kissed Jacob with more passion than she had ever before. She moved her hands to his chest, longing for the boldness to unbutton his shirt. To let him know that she wanted more. Instead of his shirt buttons, she slipped her hand under one of his suspenders, inching it toward his shoulder. His muscles tensed under her touch.

A groan escaped his lips and he pulled her onto his lap. His heartbeat pounded against her chest as his hands clumsily loosened the pins under her *kapp*.

"*Ach*, Rachel...*mei lieb*..." he whispered, his voice more of a pant. His lips moved down toward her ear, then her neck. She didn't protest when his hands roamed wherever they willed.

At this point in time, Rachel didn't care. *Nee*, she welcomed his gentle touch. It felt *wunderbaar* to be desired. To feel her hair down around her shoulders and Jacob indulging in it as though she were his *fraa*.

But she wasn't. And he wasn't her *ehemann*. Soon, he'd belong to her sister. She suddenly felt sick. "Jacob, *nee*." She sobbed, forcing herself away. "We cannot do this. You...you will be married to *mei schweschder* soon."

"I don't know if I can wait years to marry you. Rachel, I want you with everything in me. I love you."

"I know. I love you too. But we can't, Jacob."

"If only *we* were marrying in three days. I don't think I'm going to be a *gut* husband to your *schweschder*. How can I, when my thoughts will dwell with you?"

"What are we going to do?"

"The only thing we can. Pray and take one day at a time."

SIXTEEN

*J*acob couldn't help the scowl on his face as he sat at the *Eck* with his new *fraa*. He may have been compelled to marry Leah, but he was not happy about it.

Rachel had been conspicuously absent today. He didn't doubt that she was likely somewhere off by herself crying out to *Der Herr*. He felt like doing the same thing.

How was this all going to work out? Could he remain a faithful husband to Leah all the while seeing and longing for Rachel each day?

They were to make their new home in Marlin's *dawdi haus*. He'd be sleeping just a wall away from his beloved. How could he stand to be that close to her and not take her into his arms? He did not have an honest answer. It would be a temptation for sure.

As well-wishers neared their table to offer their

congratulations, all Jacob could think about was that he couldn't wait for this day—*nee*, this period of his life— to be over. He longed for the day when he'd be married to Rachel. *Ach*, if only it were Rachel sitting by his side. If it were, he had no doubt he'd be wearing a smile he couldn't contain. His heart would be full of joy instead of dread. He'd be looking forward to spending this night, and every night, lying in her arms.

Leah hadn't said much of anything. He guessed she was probably just as miffed about this situation as Jacob and Rachel were. He glanced her way and caught her sad half smile. What must it be like for a woman to be married to a man she was certain did not love her? Painful, no doubt. But Jacob couldn't help it. He couldn't just switch out his feelings. *His* choice had been Rachel, not Leah.

By the time the evening was over, Jacob was exhausted. He'd never experienced a more taxing day in his life. Nevertheless, he was glad for it to finally be over.

He glanced around the dim *dawdi haus*. There was no sense in lighting a bunch of lanterns when they were just turning in for the night.

Leah moved toward the bedroom and he heard her take something out of a drawer, then she disappeared into the adjoining bathroom.

Jacob took the opportunity to divest himself of his wedding garments and stripped down to his usual sleeping attire—his boxer shorts. He slipped into bed, but left the lantern lit on the nightstand opposite his side of the bed.

Leah emerged from the bathroom but his back was turned. He outened the lantern and the room became pitch black. Jacob heaved a sigh. This was not how he'd pictured his wedding night at all. *Nee*, he'd pictured beautiful Rachel in his arms with her long hair flowing down over her…

Nee, he should not be having those thoughts! He chastised himself. If only he could make himself fall asleep. He tossed and turned, but sleep alluded him.

Ten minutes later, he stared up at the pitch-black ceiling. He listened closely. Was Leah sobbing? *Ach*…

He turned on his side and tentatively placed a hand on her shoulder—the first time he'd actually touched his *fraa* other than holding her hand while they'd agreed to their vows.

"Leah? Are you all right?" His voice was gentle.

More sniffling. She shrugged.

"Is there something I can do for you?"

"*Nee*."

"I…" He swallowed. *Ach*, this was now his *fraa*. He was a sorry excuse for an *ehemann*. Was it his fault she was crying? Probably. Was she expecting something from him and not communicating what her needs were? Probably. He didn't love her, but he wasn't completely heartless. He lightly nudged her shoulder. "*Kumm*."

She reluctantly turned and he gathered her into his open arms. He pulled her to his chest and allowed her to cry for as long as she needed to.

He felt ashamed. He'd been so occupied with his own hurt that he hadn't even considered the pain Leah might be feeling. He'd been commanded by *Der Herr* to love his neighbor. Surely it was not an easy thing to have to marry someone who you knew didn't love you. Someone your father forced on you. Someone who was head-over-heels in love with your sister.

He smoothed her hair as her sobbing ceased. "Are you okay?"

"*Nee*, I will never be okay. I'm dying, Jacob."

Ach… He had no clue how to deal with this.

He couldn't see much in the darkness, so he used his hands to find her face. He found her lips and kissed her on the mouth and she responded in turn. But he couldn't muster the same passion he felt with Rachel. It just didn't exist. It was likely Leah's first kiss. It didn't last long. He pulled back. "Don't worry, *fraa*. You will not be alone. I will be with you."

He held her in his arms until she eventually surrendered to sleep.

Somehow, they'd learn to navigate this complicated life together. It wouldn't be easy, but he would bide his time until he could finally marry the woman of his dreams.

He closed his eyes and offered a prayer for his beloved. *Gott, please be with Rachel. Help her through this. And comfort Leah too. Help us all through this.*

Shortly thereafter, he gave in to the delicious nocturnal pull as well.

Jacob entered the kitchen, wiping the sleep from his eyes. "Smells *gut*."

Leah turned around from the stove, an uncertain smile on her face. "I...I didn't know how you like your eggs. I hope scrambled is okay."

"Scrambled is fine. I am not picky."

"Do you have a favorite way to eat them?"

"I like dippy eggs with toast, but like I said, I will eat anything."

"I am glad I have a husband that is easy to please."

He caught her eye and smiled. "And *I* am thankful for a wife that will cook for me."

He noticed a slight tinge in her cheek color. "It is my pleasure. I enjoy cooking and baking. Rachel, not so much."

Jacob pressed his lips together. He did not want Leah speaking ill of her younger sister. "We each have our own strengths and weaknesses."

"*Jah*. But it is important to be cheerful about feeding your family, ain't so?"

He couldn't really argue. Did Rachel usually complain when she had to prepare meals? Or was Leah just trying to make her look bad? *Ach*, he'd rather not dwell on that.

"Do you have plans for today?"

"We will need to help clean up, ain't not? It wonders me where my *schweschder* disappeared to yesterday."

"I'm sure it was a difficult day for her, as it was for all of us. I'm thinking she will come around when she is ready." Although he had no idea when that would be. It had to be heartbreaking knowing her beloved and her *schweschder* had united in holy matrimony.

"*Kumm*, eat." Leah called him away from the window. Rachel had been nowhere in sight.

Jacob bowed his head in silent prayer. He had no idea how this would all play out, but he had to trust *Der Herr*.

SEVENTEEN

*J*acob and Leah, along with Marlin and a few others from their family, made quick work of putting the Schmidts' home back in order. Jacob had been watching for Rachel all morning. He hadn't seen her since the day before the wedding. Where was she?

He cast his broom aside and approached Marlin. "Do you know where Rachel is?"

Marlin set down the bench he held and frowned. "You do not need to worry about Rachel. You have a *fraa* to tend to."

Jacob clenched his fists. What game was Marlin playing now? "Where is Rachel?" He said the words through gritted teeth.

"Not here. In Ohio."

"Ohio?" He practically shouted the word. He didn't care that everyone in the room stopped what they were doing and stared at him and Marlin. "What in *der velt*

111

is she doing in Ohio?"

"She's staying with a relative. It will give you and your *fraa* a chance to get to know each other without distractions."

Jacob felt like lifting the bench in front of him and hurling it through one of the windows across the room. "This is not what we agreed to. You promised me Rachel!"

"And you will have her. When it is time." He frowned. "Keep your voice down, *sohn*."

"When is she coming back?" Did his voice sound as desperate as he felt?

"That is to be determined."

"Why? Why did you send her away, Marlin? Do you have any idea what this is doing to her?" What it was doing to him?

"It is best."

"Did she *want* to go to Ohio?"

"She agreed to it."

"Kind of like I agreed to marry Leah?"

"*Chust* enjoy your *fraa*. Be a *gut ehemann*. Make her smile. Leah deserves to smile. She has been through much."

Ach... He felt so bad that Leah was stuck in the middle of this. He had to remind himself that she was a real person with real feelings and emotions too.

"You are disgracing your *fraa* by mentioning her *schweschder* in the presence of others, ain't so?"

He glanced over at Leah, his *fraa*. She cleaned the window, but her expression was nothing like a new wife's should be. He didn't want her to feel bad. He didn't want *anybody* to feel bad. He just wanted to see Rachel, his beloved. He wanted to know she was still waiting in the wings for him. He *needed* to know. He *needed* to see her.

"When will Rachel be back? I need her here. I need to see her. You know the only reason I agreed to marrying Leah is because you promised me Rachel. You *promised* me, Marlin."

"She will be back in two weeks."

"Two weeks?" His voice screeched. "*Nee*, that's not acceptable."

"Two weeks." He repeated firmly.

Ach, he hadn't gone without seeing Rachel more than a couple of days since they'd met. It seemed like sheer torture. His heart raced. What if Marlin was lying? What if this was all a plot to get Leah married off and he'd never see Rachel again?

"I want a phone number. I want to talk to her."

"*Nee*."

"Marlin, *please*." He'd resort to begging if he had to. "I knew I never should have agreed to this."

Marlin's eyes flickered toward where Leah was

working. "Keep your voice down."

"I'm leaving. I can't do this. I'm filing for an annulment. Today." He pushed past Marlin and stormed outside.

"Jacob." He heard Marlin calling him, but he ignored his words. "Jacob, wait!"

He kept walking until Marlin tackled him to the ground.

"Get off me!" He was so frustrated at this point, he actually considered striking his father-in-law.

"*Nee. Nee.* Do not do this."

"I will. I cannot live without my Rachel. I'll find her, even if I have to knock on every door in Ohio."

"I'll have a driver bring her home tomorrow, if you will reconsider."

"Tomorrow?"

"Tomorrow. You have my word."

"Fine." He shoved his father-in-law off him, then walked away. He needed to get as far away from this place as his feet would carry him, because he was at the end of his emotional rope.

"Where are you going?"

"For a walk. I need to clear my head."

"*Ach*, okay. I'll let your *fraa* know so she doesn't worry."

She should be worried. Because Jacob was tired of Marlin's games. He didn't like being a pawn.

EIGHTEEN

After much introspection and thoughtful prayer, *Der Herr* had convicted Jacob's heart. Whether he liked it or not, the reality was that he was not married to Rachel, but to Leah. Leah Schmidt. *Nee*, Leah King now. Jacob's Leah, she'd likely be called. And at least for the next several years, Lord willing.

He needed to step up, be a man, and take responsibility.

Jacob admitted to himself that he had no clue what he was doing. How could he be a *gut* husband to Leah and still remain steadfast and faithful in his love for Rachel?

He pulled his Bible onto his lap, fingering the pages to find the concordance. Husband. That was the key word he was searching for.

He realized that he could not do this without help from *Der Herr*. He thumbed through the references.

Ach, there were many, but most did not seem to apply to him.

Gott, give me understanding and wisdom.

His eyes roamed the verses. *Let the husband render unto the wife due benevolence: and likewise also the wife unto the husband.*

What did that even mean? Due benevolence? He sighed. He'd need a dictionary for sure.

He went in search of one, but the only books he saw were the typical books found in most Amish homes. A German Bible, a prayer book, an *Ausbund*, and *Martyr's Mirror*. He didn't think there was a dictionary in the *dawdi haus*, but perhaps there was one in the main dwelling.

But did he want to enter the house and risk seeing Rachel? He nearly laughed at himself. When did he *not* want to see Rachel? *Ach*, he saw her in his dreams. But he should not be dreaming of her. He mentally chastised himself. *Nee*, he should be dreaming of his *fraa*.

He hurried through the adjoining door into the big house. All was quiet. He went to the bookshelf and spotted the dictionary immediately. He returned to the *dawdi haus* unnoticed. Not that he was sneaking. *Nee*, he was welcome in Marlin's home anytime.

Benevolence. The disposition to do good. To show a

kindness. Desire to promote another's happiness.

Ach, so it meant it was his duty to be kind to his *fraa* and make her happy? And the same was true for her, according to the verse.

This was going to be more challenging than he expected. Perhaps the other verses would explain more. His gaze dropped back to his Bible.

The wife hath not power of her own body, but the husband: and likewise also the husband hath not power of his own body, but the wife.

Defraud ye not one the other, except it be with consent for a time, that ye may give yourselves to fasting and prayer; and come together again, that Satan tempt you not for your incontinency.

Oh, great. What did incontinency mean? He might understand from the text, but he'd better look it up just to be sure.

Incontinency. Lack of bodily self-control.

Ach, that made sense. So this was referring to the marriage bed, it seemed. And while, prior to his forced marriage, many times he'd imagined sharing the marriage bed with Rachel. But not with Leah.

According to *Der Herr's* Word, this was his Christian duty.

But what about other aspects of marriage? The normal day to day stuff.

He turned back to his concordance to find the other verses that referenced a husband. *Ephesians*. *Ach*, there seemed to be quite a bit.

He skimmed over it...*husband head of the wife*...*Husbands, love your wives, even as Christ loved the church, and gave himself for it...sanctify and cleanse it with the washing of water by the word...so ought men to love their wives as their own bodies...so love his wife even as himself...*

Ach, that was a tall order.

He moved to the next reference, again skimming. *Colossians. Husbands, love your wives, and be not bitter against them.*

Nee, he wasn't bitter against Leah. But he had to admit being a little bitter against Marlin. *Forgive me, Lord. I know it is not right to be bitter against Marlin either.*

He glanced down at the Bible again. *1 Peter...husbands, dwell with them according to knowledge, giving honour unto the wife, as unto the weaker vessel...that your prayers be not hindered.*

Jacob finally closed the Bible and sighed deeply. He never realized how much responsibility came with being a husband.

So, he was to love her as himself, share their marriage bed often, read *Gott's* Word with her, not harbor bitterness against her, offer kindness toward her, seek her good over his, know her.

He hung his head. *Gott, I don't know if I can be all these things for mei fraa. Especially when my heart belongs to Rachel. But I want to follow you, Herr Gott. I want to do this Your way and receive Your blessings. Please bless our union as husband and wife. And help Rachel come to terms with what is here and now. Help us both to have patience so we may come together in Your perfect time. And help mei fraa, Leah. We have difficult days ahead with her illness. Help me to be the man she needs me to be and to love her like You loved the church. Amen.*

Jacob thought on all he'd read. How could he show his *fraa* a kindness? *Ach*, he'd have to think on that one. Hopefully, *Der Herr* would show him when the time was right.

NINETEEN

*J*acob reclined at the table, while Leah gathered the dishes from supper. "*Denki* for supper."

"You are welcome. Will you be ready for dessert soon? I made zucchini applesauce bread. Rachel said you really liked when I made it last time."

Rachel… Ach, nee, he wouldn't think about her now. "I do. It was delicious. *Denki*. But I don't think I am ready for it yet."

Show her a kindness. "*Jah*." He nodded.

She turned slightly, lifting a brow. "What was that?"

"*Ach*, nothing." He looked around to find something to do. "Is…is there a towel I could use to clean the table with?"

She spun around and stared at him as though he were the most peculiar thing she'd ever seen. "*Ach…jah*." She fished inside a drawer, removed a washcloth, and handed it to him.

He ran it under the faucet, then wrung it out, and proceeded to wipe the table clean.

"You don't have to help me." Her voice was quiet.

"I want to." He emptied the crumbs into the trash can, then rinsed the rag. "Where should I put this? I just rinsed it out."

She began filling one of the sinks with water. "I will clean it with dish soap and use it for the dishes."

He stood next to her and she eyed him curiously.

"You don't mind if I help with dishes, do you?" He waggled his eyebrows.

"You don't need to. I can do it."

"I know you can. But I wish to show you a kindness." Besides, when Leah got sick, he'd likely be doing all the chores himself. It wouldn't hurt to have some practice.

The stare was back. Her mouth opened then closed again. Had he rendered her speechless? Apparently so.

Jacob smiled to himself. This 'showing a kindness' thing seemed to be working pretty well so far.

"*Denki*," she whispered.

"*Kumm, fraa*." Jacob patted the place next to him on the couch. He tried to keep a mental list of all the things he'd read that he wanted to incorporate into their marriage. His duties as a Christian husband.

Leah placed the drying towel down on the kitchen counter, then quietly heeded his call. She sat on the couch, but too far away for his thinking.

"You may *kumm* closer. I was reading today and I wanted to show you what I read." He pulled his Bible from the small table next to the couch. He held it up. "Do you read this?"

"*Nee*. Not really." At least she was honest.

Although, he wasn't quite sure how the leaders in this district felt about studying the Bible at home on one's own. Especially the *Englisch* Bible Larry had given him. It might be *verboten*. He wouldn't ask.

"I was praying today, asking *Der Herr* for wisdom on being a *gut ehemann*."

Her eyes widened. "You prayed for...for *us*?"

"*Jah*. I know our situation is not ideal, not what we planned for, but we can make the best of it, ain't so? I want to have a *gut* marriage. Do you want that too?"

She nodded. "*Jah*."

He proceeded to read the verses he'd read earlier that day. "That is how I want to be. To be in *Gott's* will."

"That is what I want too."

They were making progress, but this was still so

awkward. It seemed like he and Rachel had just clicked immediately. There was a mutual attraction and it only grew the more they'd spent time together as they shared their hopes and dreams. But with Leah, every little step felt forced. He knew in his head what he should do, how he should act, but his heart couldn't help but long for Rachel.

Ach, he *had to* stop comparing Leah to Rachel. He had to. If he didn't, he'd always find flaws in his *fraa*. And that wasn't loving her as Christ loved the church and it certainly wasn't showing a kindness.

Love her for who she *is*. The thought came out of nowhere.

He thought of his mental list. He'd showed her kindness by helping in the kitchen. He'd read *Der Herr's* Word with her. What else was there? Oh yeah, the part about the marriage bed. He gulped.

Ach…

He'd always imagined his first intimate moments would be with his beloved Rachel. The thought that they wouldn't be bereaved him. *Ach, stop thinking about Rachel!* He chastised himself. He'd never be a *gut* husband if he was always thinking of someone other than his *fraa*.

He swallowed, eyeing his *fraa*. How would she feel if he made physical advances? Only one way to find out.

She had responded to his kiss on their wedding night. That was something encouraging.

He reached for her hand, then tugged her near. She scooted closer to him, her gaze curious. He reached over and caressed her cheek, then leaned forward and met her lips with his.

Again, she responded to his kiss.

"*Kumm,*" he mumbled.

He pulled her onto his lap to kiss her more thoroughly, his fingers weaving through her hair. He leaned back to see and untied the kerchief that covered her head, then found the pins that held her hair in place, loosening her tresses from the confines of her bun.

Her eager hands indicated she was enjoying his advances, as they roamed his neck, arms, and chest.

He tentatively caressed her in turn, as a husband should, and a surprised but welcoming gasp escaped her lips. This was actually kind of fun, he admitted to himself.

"Leah," he murmured, "Do you want to—"

A knock sounded at the door.

Jacob grunted in frustration and Leah leaped off his lap. Had they even locked the door? He moved toward the entrance as she headed toward the bedroom, no doubt to make herself presentable for company.

Jacob was prepared to tell whoever it was to come

back tomorrow. He jerked the door open, still in a bit of a daze. "Rachel?" His eyes widened.

A puzzled look crossed her features, then her gaze swept over him, examining his attire. She stumbled backward and gasped.

He glanced down at where her eyes focused. *Ach*, he hadn't realized that Leah had unfastened a couple of the buttons on his shirt, and had apparently started on his broadfalls as well. His cheeks burned. "I...uh...we..."

Ach, this was awkward. He shouldn't have hurried to the door in a rush. He should have looked himself over. He chastised himself for his carelessness.

"I see it took you a whole ten seconds to get over me!" Tears immediately shimmered in her eyes as she spun around and ran off.

"Rachel, wait..." He sighed. But he didn't go after her.

What could he say? That he was enjoying a little physical time with his *fraa*? That he was trying his best to be a *gut* husband to her *schweschder*? Physical intimacy was expected between a husband and wife.

Help, Gott. I don't know what I'm doing.

Leah emerged from the bedroom, her hair neatly in place once again. "Do we have company? I can put some coffee on."

"*Nee*, it was Rachel. She left without saying what

she wanted." He shrugged.

An unspoken sorrow seemed to pass between them.

Leah sighed, lowered her eyes to the floor, then moved to the kitchen. Away from him. No doubt she felt his rejection at the sound of her *schweschder's* name. "Would you…would you like some dessert now?"

He forced out a breath and frowned, frustrated with himself. He shouldn't have answered the door. Not only had their intimate moment vanished, but he'd traumatized Rachel as well.

"*Jah*, that sounds *gut*." Well, at least he could still look forward to dessert.

Dessert he could do. Trying to keep a balance between himself, Leah, and Rachel was questionable. But he couldn't just give up. He had to try, didn't he? He had no control over the situation with Rachel. But with Leah…

Nee. They weren't going to do this. They'd been interrupted. So what.

"*Nee*, forget the dessert." He took three purposeful steps, until he stood face to face with her. He emptied her hands of the zucchini applesauce bread, placing the plates on the counter beside her, then stepped even closer until she had nowhere to retreat to. He cradled her face in his hands, pressing himself against her, and kissed her on the mouth with the same passion they'd left off at when the knock sounded on the door. He then swiftly lifted her into his arms and carried her to their marriage bed.

Dessert would have to wait.

TWENTY

Rachel stormed away from the *dawdi haus* and toward the fields. *Dat* would just have to be patient for his pie. Pie she had been about to invite Jacob and Leah to enjoy with her and *Dat*. Jacob's favorite. But apparently, *they'd* been enjoying something else.

Ach, just seeing that look on Jacob's face… She couldn't pinpoint exactly what it was at the time. Not until she glanced at his disheveled clothing.

She closed her eyes against the barrage of tears that couldn't be stopped. Jacob had never looked at her that way—like she was an interloper, unwelcomed, a stranger, an imposition. *Never*.

His eyes had always lit up at the mere sight of her, as though she were the most wonderful thing he'd ever seen in all the world. As though she were the sun and the moon and the stars together in all their glory. He'd always been overeager to see her. Head-over-heels in love. Hopelessly in love. With her. And her alone.

But *now*?

Nee, he certainly hadn't been thinking of *her*. She was likely the furthest thing from his mind prior to the moment he'd thrust the door open like the *haus* was on fire. *Nee*, the *haus* had not been on fire. *He* had been.

She shook when a sob overtook her body.

Hurt and frustration and anger and resentment coursed through her entire being. She could hardly breathe when she thought of what she'd interrupted. As a matter of fact, right now they were probably…

Nee. Nee. She shook her head. This is not how it was supposed to be.

A team of Percherons must have settled right on top of her chest. Maybe, if they crushed her completely, she'd be put out of her misery.

She couldn't abide the thought of Jacob—*her* beloved—sharing his love with another. How could she stand seeing the two of them day after day? Happily married. When it should have rightly been her.

Ach, she hated her father for what he'd done to them. Why couldn't he have found another *ehemann* for Leah? Why did he have to steal *her* beloved away? It wasn't fair in any sense of the word.

This was a heartache she didn't think she'd ever get

over. It would likely be the death of her. Did people actually die of broken hearts?

Leah's cheeks appeared to glow the following morning as she prepared breakfast at the stove. She'd barely glanced back at Jacob, likely embarrassed. She had enjoyed their intimate moments just as much as he had, but he could certainly understand her inhibition in the morning light.

Ach, they were practically strangers. He supposed it was a normal thing for couples to feel this way during their first days and perhaps weeks of marriage.

They never did get back to their dessert. Although, it was no longer on the table when he'd awoken for chores before dawn, so Leah must've put it away sometime during the night.

He'd slept like a *boppli*.

A silly satisfied grin played on his lips when he entertained thoughts of the previous evening. Perhaps they could experience a similar one tonight. Minus the interruption, that is. *Ach*…

"Do you have any plans for today?" He smiled as she set a mug of steaming coffee in front of him.

"Nothing out of the ordinary. I'll figure out our meals, make some bread, maybe work in the garden." She shrugged. "I don't think we have enough dirty clothes for a load of laundry yet."

He nodded. "I'll be working at the shop today." He'd been off since before the wedding.

"Okay."

"I will leave the phone number in case you need to get ahold of me for whatever reason. If I'm ever late home, check the phone shanty for a message."

"Okay."

He reached for her hand and squeezed it gently. He winked. "I had a *gut* time last *nacht*."

His comment sent all kinds of color flooding to her cheeks. "I…I'll get breakfast."

She rose from the table, then set a large plate of dippy eggs on the table, along with toast and sausage.

He gazed at his *fraa* in wonder. Was she trying to show him a kindness as well? Meet his needs, fulfill his desires?

He grinned, then bowed his head for silent prayer. It was turning out to be a wonderful day indeed.

Rachel tensed when Leah entered the *haus*. Why was her *schweschder* here? Hadn't she already moved all her things to the *dawdi haus* prior to the wedding? She had no need to be in the main dwelling.

No matter. She didn't need to acknowledge her.

"Is *Dat* here?" Leah asked from behind her.

She continued washing dishes, but shrugged her shoulders.

Leah sighed loudly. "Does that mean you don't know or you don't want to tell me?"

She gritted her teeth. The fewer words she spoke, the better. "Not in here. Probably outside."

"Fine." By the sound of it, she walked outside, then shut the door.

Gut. After that last embarrassing ordeal, Rachel decided it would probably be best to avoid Jacob and Leah at all costs. Although it pained her not to see Jacob, seeing him—especially like she had yesternight—was far worse.

TWENTY-ONE

*J*acob glanced out the window. *Ach*, Rachel was heading into the barn. He hadn't seen her around in a couple of days. Not even out with her sheep. Was she allowing him and Leah some time for privacy? Or was it something else?

After the day she'd knocked on their door, then ran away...

Ach, he had to catch her. He needed to try to smooth things over. Somehow.

"I'll be right back, Leah." Jacob rushed outside.

He hastened his steps toward the barn and called out before she stepped inside. "Rachel!"

She paused for a slight second, then continued around the side of the barn instead of going inside. *Ach*, was she ignoring him?

"Rachel, wait!" He wasn't sure whether she'd heeded his call or not, because she was beyond his view.

He rounded the corner as she was just about to go around back. "Rachel! Wait, please!" *Ach*, she *was* avoiding him. He jogged toward her and grasped her arm, then spun her to face him.

She yanked her arm free. "Don't, Jacob!" Tears clouded her eyes.

"*Ach, lieb.*"

"*Nee*, don't call me *lieb*. I'm not your *lieb* anymore. I'm your *schweschder* now." Her chin quivered.

"*Ach*, Rachel. You will always be *mei lieb. Mei schatzi.*"

"*Nee*." She refused to look him in the eye. "You have a *fraa* now. You are part of a marriage. A marriage *I* am *not* part of."

His heart crumbled at her words. She wasn't giving up on them, was she? "Rachel, I agreed to marry your *schweschder* for you. For us. She is only a means to an end."

He regretted his choice of words the moment they escaped, although they were true, ain't not? It was a *gut* thing Leah had not heard them. If she had, their union would have seemed meaningless. Which it wasn't. Not really. He enjoyed his *fraa*, he admitted to himself.

"I hate it. I hate seeing you two together. I know you are going to fall in love with her. You will forget about me."

"*Nee*. Never. I will always love you, Rachel. You are my first love. And I have every intention of marrying you. Someday."

"And you do not think you will give your heart to her after living with her for many years?"

"*Ach*, Rachel…" The fact was, he was already developing some feelings for Leah. But it wasn't love. Not yet. They *were* husband and wife, after all. He swallowed.

"So I am right, then?" She crossed her arms across her chest stiffly and eyed him. "Have you…?" She let the unspoken words dangle in the air.

He thought of the night they'd first shared their marriage bed and several other times after that. He looked away. He sighed. "Rachel…"

"I knew it. I knew this would happen."

"I don't know what to do. How to make this work between us. I love you, but I am married to Leah. I will likely have *bopplin* with her and even come to love her. But that does not mean I will stop loving you. My love for you will never die, Rachel."

Rachel looked up at Jacob. Saw the torment in his eyes. She wanted to believe his words. Really she did. "I…I thought I could do this. Stand by and watch you and *mei schweschder*. But I can't, Jacob. Every time I see the two of you, my heart rips in pieces." Soon, it would be shredded beyond repair. *Ach*, she hated her cursed tears.

Pain clamped down on her heart like one of the traps her father set for the wild animals that threatened their livelihood.

"So, what do you want to do?" He frowned. "Do you...do you want to..." He swallowed, struggling to get his words out. "Do you want to see other men?"

Nee, I only want to see you, Jacob. I've only ever wanted to see you. Was he releasing her from their promise? "Is that what you want?"

"*Nee*. But I want you to be happy. And if you're not, then..." He sighed heavily. "*Ach*, Rachel. This is *sehr* hard, ain't so?"

"*Jah*, it's hard." She pivoted. "I...I don't know, Jacob. Maybe it would be better if I kept attending the gatherings."

"You're not giving up on us, are you?" She heard the misery in his voice. "Because if you are..." His fingers troweled through his hair. "*Ach*, Rachel, I couldn't bear it. I would not have married your *schweschder* if it wasn't for the promise of you. You are the light at the end of my covered bridge." He chuckled. "*Ach*, that was cheesy."

"*Jah*, it was." She giggled.

"But you know what I mean." He raised a hand and caressed her cheek. *Ach*, how she wished he'd dip his head and kiss her senseless like in times past. Instead he stepped away. "You are my everything, Rachel."

TWENTY-TWO

It was pure misery. Not only had he been coerced into marrying a woman he didn't love, now he was forced to stand by while other young men sought out his beloved. Hadn't Marlin promised Jacob?

Jacob scowled as Elmer Miller carried on a conversation with Rachel. They talked, they laughed, and then they'd left together in his courting buggy. *Nee*, Rachel could not be courted by anyone else. He couldn't lose her for sure and for certain. Any young man could see what a fine catch she was.

But he couldn't go after her either. His *fraa* was present along with everyone else in the *g'may*.

Although he'd married Leah on the contingency that he'd have the opportunity to marry Rachel at a future date, he'd never consider being unfaithful to his *fraa*. It was just something he wouldn't do, no matter how much he longed for her sister.

It was like he and Rachel had to put their relationship on hold for an undetermined amount of time. An intermission of sorts. But what if Rachel fell in love with Elmer or some other young man? *Ach*, he wouldn't be able to bear it.

Jacob admitted to himself that he was outright spying. He had to. Someone had to make sure that Elmer Miller kept his hands to himself as he and Rachel sat out on the porch swing.

But what if he didn't? What if he attempted to kiss Rachel?

It wasn't like Jacob could just pop his head around the corner of the house and yell, "Stop!"

He knew the reason Rachel had decided to let other young men court her. He'd read it in her eyes when she'd glanced over and had seen him and Leah holding hands. He hoped she wasn't trying to make him jealous, but if she was, it was definitely working.

She was his future *fraa*. He had a right to be jealous, didn't he?

Ach, watching the two of them laughing and talking equated to torture of the worst kind. He couldn't stand to lose her to someone else.

Relief flooded his entire being when Elmer left with not so much as a peck on the cheek. As soon as his buggy was out of sight, Rachel turned to go inside.

"Rachel!" He whispered loudly.

She let out a small peep. "Jacob, you startled me. What are you doing out here?"

"I...uh...I heard the buggy." He grimaced. "Listen, Rachel. I know it hurt you to see Leah and me—"

"You love her, don't you?" Rachel frowned.

"She is *mei fraa. Der Herr* commands me to." *Ach*, Jacob despised the position Marlin had put him in.

Tears glistened in Rachel's eyes. "I knew it. I knew I was going to lose you."

"Shh...*kumm*." He spread his arms wide and she stepped into his embrace. "You have *not* lost me. I am still here." *Ach*, how he wished that he could press his lips to hers, to show her how much he loved her. But he was married to her sister now and to do so would be wrong. He gently rubbed her back instead.

"Jacob, what are you—" Leah's eyes flew wide.

Jacob and Rachel immediately broke apart. Guilt tore at his heart. This situation wasn't fair to any of them.

He stared at his *fraa*. Had she changed out of her nightgown? "Leah, I...uh, I thought you were in bed

143

already." Shame filled him.

Leah pinned her sister with a menacing glare. "What are you doing? Are you trying to steal my husband from me?"

"Jacob doesn't love you. He loves me. He wanted to marry *me*."

"*Nee. I* am the one who shares his marriage bed. *I* am the one who will give him *bopplin*."

Jacob gritted his teeth.

"Only because *Dat* forced him. He would have *never* chosen you willingly."

Jacob had to step in. Rachel's words were likely true, although he wouldn't say *never*, but they were hurtful. He could see the pain in his *fraa's* eyes. "Rachel, *nee*. Please, do not fight. I hate to see what this has done to you. You two are sisters. You were friends before the wedding."

"A friend does not steal away your intended." Rachel glowered at her sister.

"I did not steal anything. You said it yourself. The only reason Jacob married me is so he could have you. I know he doesn't care for me like he does for you." Moisture sprang to her eyes. "Now, you all are just waiting around until I die."

"*Ach*, Leah." Jacob placed his hand on her shoulder. She shrugged it off. "It's true and we all know it."

Rachel's lips pressed together. "I am upset, but I do not wish my sister dead. I just wish things were different, that's all."

"Don't I deserve a little happiness too? I know I am not Jacob's first choice." She laughed bitterly. "I'm nobody's choice. I wish I never even survived my childhood."

"*Ach*, Leah. Do not think like that. Don't say those words." Jacob frowned. *Nee*, she wasn't his first choice, but he had developed feelings for her. He tried to show her love, whether he felt it or not. *Nee*, they didn't go as deep as his feelings for her sister but at least they'd been able to form somewhat of a friendship, a mutual respect for each other as spouses. He hoped Rachel's words hadn't undermined that.

"Is it true? What Rachel said earlier?" Leah changed back into her nightgown and pulled the quilt over her body.

Jacob stared at her. "Which part?"

"That you do not love me."

He slipped into bed beside her.

"*Nee*. I do love you. Have I not shown it?" He

reached for a renegade hair strand and moved it off her brow.

"You have." She frowned. "Yet I find Rachel in your arms. You still love her, ain't so?"

"*Jah*, I cannot help it. I will always love Rachel. I will still marry her one day, *Gott* willing."

"Do you still wish you'd married her instead of me? Of course, you do, what a *dumm* question for me to ask. I…I just hoped…"

"Leah…don't. Don't do this."

"I know you do. I can see it in your eyes every time she is near. I can hear it in your voice when you speak." Tears surfaced and rolled down her cheeks. "I share your marriage bed, but I will never have your heart, will I?"

"*Ach*, Leah…" He ached to reach over and dry her tears, but he sensed she wouldn't allow it.

"You will not admit it, but I know that it is true."

"This was not my doing. You know how it went. I intended to marry your *schweschder*. Your *vatter* insisted I marry you."

"I'd rather have remained an *alt maedel* than to have a husband that is in love with someone else."

"I don't know what to say or do to make this right, Leah. I am sorry." To deny his love for Rachel would be a lie.

"*Jah, vell*, I am too. You have no idea how much it

hurts me to see the way you look at *mei schweschder*. I wish you'd look at me like that. Just once."

Ach, what could he say? That he wasn't attracted to her the same way he was to Rachel? That he hadn't even really known her at all before they wed? He'd been making an effort to change that.

"I cannot help it. I really am trying to be a *gut* husband to you. It is hard to deny my feelings for Rachel. My heart has yearned for her since I first saw her. We courted for almost a year. We'd planned to marry. I thought we would marry, up until the day your *vatter* published the *banns*." He sighed. "I don't know my place. I cannot please everyone at the same time. But I'm trying, Leah. I'm trying to be the *ehemann* you need me to be. Do you regret marrying me?"

"I'm trying not to. Do you?"

"I don't. I'm anxious to see what *Der Herr* has planned for our future. I know that Rachel is likely my distant future, but right now, *our* present is what I am trying to focus on. I don't want to fret about the future. It is in *Der Herr's* hands. Let's live for what is now, *jah*?" Now, he reached over and brushed away her remaining tears.

"*Jah*, we will try to do that. I will do my best to trust in *Gott's* plan."

"*Gut*." He leaned toward his wife, claimed her lips, and loved her as a husband should.

TWENTY-THREE

*J*acob had been studying his *fraa* lately. Something was definitely wrong. He noticed she'd been more tired, and pallor marked her appearance. Surely her time to expire hadn't come yet. It was too soon.

Gott, please no. Please keep her alive long enough to find joy in life.

Ach, he wasn't ready to let her go. He'd come to love and cherish her.

Was he being disloyal to Rachel? Perhaps. But when in contrast to his *fraa's* very life being snatched away, spending time with Rachel had to take second place. Could one even put value on a life? *Nee*, he didn't think so.

Leah didn't think she was worthy of love. Did she equate outer beauty with inner worth? *Jah*, no one would deny her sister Rachel was beautiful— downright drop-dead gorgeous to Jacob's thinking. But

Leah possessed her own beauty. Didn't *Der Herr* say He had made everything beautiful in His time?

As though summoned by his thoughts, Leah walked into the room. She did not look herself. Didn't look *gut* at all. She should probably be in bed.

"Leah, I think you need to go lie down, *schatzi*."

"Jacob, I…" she struggled for a breath "…I…"

Jacob swooped in just in time to catch her in his arms. He immediately picked her up and carried her to their bedroom.

"Leah, are you all right?" It was a silly question. Of course she wasn't all right.

He smoothed back a strand of her hair then bent down and pressed his lips to her brow. Worry crashed down on him, nearly suffocating him with fear. He needed to pray.

He took Leah's limp hand in his. "Dear Lord *Gott*, please be with my precious Leah, my *fraa*. Give her strength. Give her health. And please, *Gott*, give me wisdom."

Her eyes were closed. He sighed in relief when he noticed her chest rise and fall.

"I'm going to call a driver. I need you to stay right here. Don't try to get up." He was unsure if she was even conscious to hear or understand his words. "Okay, *lieb*?" He caressed her face once more, kissed her cheek, then ran outside as though the house were on fire.

"Jacob! What's wrong?" Marlin called, stepping out from the barn.

"Please, go call a driver. It's Leah! She needs to see the doctor."

Confident that Marlin would do as asked, Jacob rushed back inside. He didn't want to leave his *fraa's* side for a moment longer than necessary.

Rachel's heart pounded as she walked the hospital corridor. She'd left *Dat* in the waiting room. They still hadn't received any word as to Leah's condition, which made her worry even more.

She pushed open the door to Leah's room. And was totally unprepared for the sight before her.

Leah lay sleeping on the small hospital bed. Jacob had crawled up next to her, his arm draped around her. His eyes appeared to be closed, whether in sleep or prayer, she didn't know. If it had been *anyone* other than the man she loved, she would have thought the sight endearing. Precious even. Instead, pain filled her heart.

Jacob obviously *loved* her sister. There was no denying it.

Before her tears could fall, she did an about face and vacated the room as quickly as possible. As soon as she stumbled upon an empty nearby waiting room, she sank down into a hard plastic chair and wept.

"Shh…" She felt a comforting arm drape around her shoulders. "It'll be okay." It was Jacob's voice.

Ach, she wished he didn't have to see her in this state. She looked terrible when she cried. Which seemed like all she ever did lately while in Jacob's presence.

"I'm sorry, it's just…" She couldn't even get the words out.

"It's all right. You don't have to cry for her. Your *schweschder* will be okay."

She frowned up at him. *Ach*, he thought she was crying for Leah? *Jah*, he would. He was oblivious to her pain. It figured.

"What is wrong with her?" She managed to sound concerned. She *should* sound concerned, and under normal circumstances she would have been.

One side of his mouth curled up. *Ach*, he was so handsome. His new beard only added to his attractiveness. "Leah is in the *familye* way. We are going to have a *boppli*."

"A…a…" She couldn't breathe. *Nee*, this could not be happening. It. Could. Not. Be.

Rachel leaped from the chair and ran out of the room as hastily as she could. Hopefully, Jacob would not come after her. Because, other than Leah, he was the last person she wanted to see right now.

Ach, she hated them all!

Why in the world was she still waiting for Jacob? He evidently didn't care about her. She had to be about the biggest *dummkopp* in the world. No doubt she was the laughing stock of the community. She really needed to just move on and find somebody else, someone who would love her.

She needed to forget about Jacob.

Because loving someone when they did not love you in return was misery, pure and simple.

TWENTY-FOUR

*J*acob had never felt so torn. *Ach*, he truly loved them both!

Leah, in a more gentle, friendly, practical way that had been born of being thrown together and doing life together day in and day out. She'd be birthing his *boppli* soon, his own flesh and blood. He couldn't not love her.

But he also loved Rachel. In a pulse-pounding, heart-racing way from the first moment he'd laid eyes on her. From that evening on, each day with her solidified his love. It had grown from irresistible, instant attraction to an easy friendship filled with laughter and passionate kisses—until he and Leah were forced into marriage. *Ach*, but he missed those heated kisses with Rachel, the intimate moments they'd shared. He missed their easy natural friendship. He really shouldn't because he felt it was a betrayal to his *fraa*, but he couldn't help it. They'd been *so* close to marriage. So close to fulfilling the passion that raged inside. So close to fulfilling his dream of being hitched to the love of his life for always.

Until it didn't happen. His world had shattered that day.

His love for Rachel would never die. It was an unquenchable forest fire that could not be put out no matter how many gallons of water it was doused with. He'd desire Rachel as his *fraa* till the day he died. She made his heart sing.

But he really, really needed to get his head on straight right now. *Ach*, he was going to be a *Dat*!

This life was crazy wonderful and frustrating at the same time.

He didn't know if Leah and Rachel would ever get along again, and that saddened him. But he'd never hold a grudge against Leah or Rachel for their rivalry. They were just as innocent in this situation as he was. He wondered if Marlin had any idea of the rift his scheme had caused between his *dochdern*. Had he thought it worth it?

Jacob sighed. Somehow, they'd figure this life and all its trials out. For now, he had to give his cares over to *Der Herr* and encourage the *maed*—well, Leah anyway, because Rachel wasn't speaking to him—to do the same. Surely *Gott* would help them through it.

Rachel grumbled to herself as she thought of Jacob and Leah. Their *boppli* would come soon. And it would be *her* niece or nephew. She might even be called on to babysit. Meaning, she'd be in regular contact with all three of them.

The happy family.

She squeezed her eyes closed, wetting her lashes as she did. *Ach*, this life was so hard.

If she didn't find something to do with herself, she'd go crazy waiting for Jacob. Who knew how long it would be before they could resume their relationship? It would likely be many, many years before they would be able to marry. If they even married at all.

She couldn't think of anything more heart-wrenching than watching your beloved love another person.

She thought of the time Elmer Stutzman had courted her. Jacob had been lurking around the corner. Watching to see if Elmer would make moves on her, no doubt. He'd been jealous. Here he was, married to Leah and he was jealous of the young men courting *her*. Perhaps he did still love her.

Nevertheless, she'd made a decision. She would begin to see other men. If she waited until Jacob was finally ready, she'd likely be an *alt maedel* and no one would want her. She still young enough to where single men still looked her way. Often. *Jah*, she'd take advantage of that. And this time, she'd allow her heart to explore the possibility of new love.

Because, while Jacob and Leah were busy creating their happy little family, she was entitled to some happiness too. Wasn't she? No one would fault her for seeking to have a love of her own. Besides, was it really fair to Leah to have a husband who loved her half-heartedly? If Rachel were to find love with someone else, perhaps Jacob would release her. Perhaps he would release himself. Then they could each fully love another.

She frowned. Who was she kidding? She couldn't possibly love someone the way she loved Jacob. Could she?

It was time to find out.

158

"Jacob!" Leah called out. Her voice sounded distressed.

He quickly towel dried his body, then poked his head through the bathroom door. "*Jah*?"

"*Kumm*! I…I need you to fetch the midwife."

The midwife? Ach… "*Jah*, okay, I'll be…just let me get dressed."

He quickly threw his trousers on and rushed to the bedroom for his shirt.

He squatted where Leah lay on the couch. He took her hand and examined her face. "Are you…will you be okay here alone?"

She inhaled a sharp breath, then exhaled. "Could you have Rachel come over while you are out?"

"*Jah*, sure." He nodded, then placed a quick kiss on her cheek.

He raced out of the house, through the adjoining door into the main house. Rachel and Marlin sat at their breakfast table and looked up at him as he entered unannounced.

"It's Leah. The…the *boppli's* coming. I need to fetch the midwife. Rachel, will you go stay with her?" His eyes pled.

She nodded. "*Jah*."

"*Gut*." Jacob rushed out the back door, hitched up the buggy with record speed, then took off down the road.

Ach, his *boppli* was coming!

TWENTY-FIVE

Rachel didn't think Jacob's smile could stretch any wider. *Ach*, the *boppli* looked so tiny in her beloved's strong arms. He'd make a *gut vatter* for sure.

"Would you like to hold little Reuben?" He handed his precious bundle to her.

She took the *boppli* and held him close to her chest. *Ach*, the *boppli* was indeed *schee*. She bent down and kissed his forehead. *Ach*, he looked like Jacob.

"Our first little one." Jacob whispered in her ear.

She stared at him, then glanced at Leah lying in her bed. *Nee*, this was not her little one. She had no business claiming another *fraa's boppli* as her own. She was not part of this happy family. She was an interloper.

Rachel noted the pride in Jacob's tone. She wished she could muster the same enthusiasm for this *boppli*.

But he was a testament to the love between Jacob and Leah, not Jacob and her.

She'd go home to her house, while Leah would be the one nestled in Jacob's strong arms tonight. Leah would be the one Jacob bestowed his kisses on.

Rachel fought hard against the feelings of jealousy and envy. It wasn't right that her beloved had been stolen away from her. It wasn't right that she floundered on her own, while Leah enjoyed the benefits of a happy family with *her* Jacob as the head.

Jah, she needed to do something different. She needed to find other dreams that didn't include a life with another woman's *ehemann*. She needed to move on without Jacob.

Jacob perused the arrangements of flowers as he entered the grocery store. *Nee*, purchasing flowers wasn't typical for an Amish man, but he wanted to find some way to acknowledge the special women in his life.

The red roses were perfect for Rachel. A symbol of his undying love for her.

A colorful mixed bouquet would likely bring a smile

to Leah's face. He loved to see her smile. Colors reminded him of sunshine, and their *boppli* had already brought lots of sunshine into their lives.

He also grabbed a couple of small cards. He'd write on them later. He thought on the words he'd pen to Leah.

To my fraa and the mother of my boppli,

The sun rises and sets on your smile.

Love, Jacob

And then to Rachel. How much would be appropriate?

I dream of you often, Rachel!

Your Beloved,

Jacob

Hopefully, they'd both appreciate his gesture. A message to Leah, showing a husband's kindness. And a message to Rachel, reminding her she held his heart.

He'd sneak in and deliver both of them when no one else was around. They'd be surprised for sure. He only wished he could see the looks on their faces.

Rachel frowned when she noticed a bouquet of red roses sitting in the middle of the supper table. When had those arrived? And more importantly, who were they from?

"*Dat*?" she called out but silence echoed back. *Dat* must still be working outside. He typically stayed out till she called him in for supper.

She marched to the flowers when she spotted a small card attached to them. *Rachel*, the envelope said. The handwriting was definitely familiar. She sighed and opened the card.

I dream of you often, Rachel!
Your beloved, Jacob

Her chest heaved. *Ach*, Jacob King had to be the most thoughtful man in the world! But he was not her beloved. *Nee*, he was Leah's. This bouquet rightly belonged to her.

Why had Jacob brought this? It was not appropriate, in light of their circumstances. His *fraa* had just delivered their first *boppli*.

She thought of taking the roses over to Leah, but thought better of it. It might be best if she didn't know. *Nee*, Rachel would hide these away in her room. Not that she needed a constant reminder of what couldn't be.

Ach, why did Jacob have to go and do something wonderful like this? She'd been determined to date other men and try to fall in love with someone else. But when Jacob showed his thoughtfulness with romantic gestures such as this, it made it nearly impossible for any other man to measure up. Surely none of the men she'd be courted by would bring her red roses—a symbol of love.

Ach, Jacob. How can I ever forget about you when you constantly make me fall in love with you?

She'd have to get him alone and have a heart-to-heart chat. He needed to know her plans—that the two of them were truly over and she'd be seeking love elsewhere. It would be difficult, but it must be said.

TWENTY-SIX

Rachel knocked on the door of the *dawdi haus*, but nobody answered. She listened closely. No noise, which meant the *boppli* must be sleeping. She'd just seen Leah outside a few minutes ago, so hopefully Jacob would be inside alone. She'd try her luck.

The moment Rachel walked in through the door that adjoined the main home to the *dawdi haus*, she noticed a beautiful bouquet of flowers displayed on their table.

"Jacob," she called out in a quiet voice in case the *boppli* was sleeping. No one answered.

She glanced around, then quickly tiptoed over to the flowers and snatched up the card that sat open on the table.

To my fraa and the mother of my boppli,
The sun rises and sets on your smile.
Love, Jacob

She sighed and set the card back on the table. *Jah,*

she was sure and certain that Jacob King had to be the most thoughtful man alive.

"What are you doing in here?" Leah's voice startled her.

"I…uh…"

"You have no business being in our home uninvited, Rachel." Leah's sharp words felt like a slap on the face. "What are you doing? Trying to lure Jacob into your arms again?"

"That was uncalled for." Rachel sighed. "You don't realize how hard it is to have the man you love—the man that loved you, that you'd planned to marry—given away to someone else."

"*Nee*, I guess I wouldn't know anything about that. Would I?"

Rachel caught the bitterness in her *schweschder's* tone.

"It's not my fault that no *buwe* courted you, Leah. It's not my fault that you couldn't find an *ehemann* of your own."

"I found an *ehemann* just fine, *denki* very much. In case you forgot, Jacob married *me*."

"He doesn't love you the way he loves me." *Ach*, she shouldn't have said that. Was it even true?

"Rachel, you need to realize that the world does not revolve around you."

"I never said it did."

"Maybe not, but you sure act like it. Jacob doesn't belong to you whether you like it or not."

Rachel's lip quivered. She knew he didn't, but did Leah have to rub it in? The fact was, Jacob *had* chosen *her*. *She* was his first choice. His beloved. He'd even said so in his card.

"I'm the mother of his *boppli*." *Ach*, why did she have to keep reminding her? It was quite obvious.

"Leah, I didn't come over here to fight with you."

"Then, why did you come?"

"I needed to talk to Jacob." She walked to the door. "Please let him know."

She stepped outside before Leah could protest.

Now the ball was in Jacob's court.

TWENTY-SEVEN

Jacob took a deep breath and knocked on the door to the main house. He removed his hat, then placed it back on his head.

Marlin opened the door with a nod.

"Rachel asked to see me."

"So she did." His father-in-law frowned.

Rachel peered around Marlin. Her green dress brought out the emerald accents in her eyes. *Ach*, she was still the most gorgeous thing he'd ever laid eyes on.

His gaze flickered toward the table. The flowers he'd left earlier were no longer there. Hopefully, she hadn't tossed them in the trash receptacle.

Rachel turned to her father. "We'll be on the porch, *Dat*. I'll make coffee when I come back in."

Marlin grunted, but nodded reluctantly.

Rachel stepped outside and closed the door behind

them. "We can sit on the swing."

Jacob swallowed. How many nights had the two of them spent out on this swing? Laughing, talking, singing, and, of course, kissing. "You wanted to talk?"

She nodded and stared at her hands. He sensed that she fought back tears. "I'm releasing you from our promise."

"What? I don't want to be released, Rachel. I—"

"Think about it, Jacob. This isn't fair to any of us. It's already been over a year. My sister could very well live a full life. How many more years will pass before we can marry? Decades? It might never come. Do you *really* want to sit around waiting, hoping for your *fraa* to die? Leah deserves better than that. Your *boppli* deserves better than that.

"I'm not getting any younger, Jacob. If I'm going to find someone who will have me, it has to be before I'm an *alt maedel*. I love you, Jacob, but this just isn't going to work." She brushed away the tears on her face, but didn't look at him.

"Rachel…Wha…? Not going to…" He squeezed his eyes shut. He wouldn't cry. He. Would. Not. "Is there anything I can say to make you change your mind?"

She shook her head.

"You're giving up on us?" His words came out on a whisper. Could she sense his devastation?

"I…I plan to see other men. For real, this time. To try to find someone who can love me and me alone. Freely."

"I can hardly believe…but I…" Anger welled inside him. "Rachel, this was for you. If I had *any* doubt that you wouldn't eventually become *mei fraa*, I never would have agreed to this. I would have moved on. Moved away. Something. But I… I've really, truly lost you?" His throat felt raw. This wasn't happening.

"I can't do this anymore, Jacob."

"I thought our love was stronger than that."

"Jacob, I love you with every breath I take. But sometimes love is just not enough." She sobbed.

"Love is always enough." He spoke the words gently.

"*Nee*, not this time. Not this time, Jacob."

His arms ached to clutch her to his chest. To rub her back, her hair. To press her against him and graze her cheeks with his fingers. To kiss her into changing her mind. To assure her time would pass quickly, if she could just wait—if she could just hold on a little longer.

But even *he* didn't have that assurance. What if she was right? What if she lost her chance at happiness? Of a life-long love? While he played husband and father to Leah and their *kinner*. What if what Marlin feared for Leah became true for Rachel? She was right. It wasn't fair to her.

"*Jah*. Okay, then." They were the saddest words he'd ever uttered. Did they convey the turmoil in his heart?

He didn't know how he found the strength, especially with how heavy his chest felt, but somehow he managed to stand from the porch swing.

He took a step away from the swing.

Then another.

And he walked away from the life—the love—he'd always dreamed of.

It was at least two hours before Jacob returned to the *dawdi haus*. He couldn't go inside. Not until he and *Der Herr* had a conversation.

He'd cried out to *Gott*. Yelled at him, in fact. *Gott knew* this would happen and He hadn't stopped Jacob from marrying Leah. He hadn't prevented Marlin's interference in their lives. He demanded to know why.

Was *Der Herr* sitting up in Heaven on His holy throne laughing at him? Was He enjoying his anguish, his turmoil? It sure seemed like it.

Jacob received an answer, but it was not the one he wanted. What he wanted from *Der Herr* was to rewind the last year and a half and place Rachel at the marriage ceremony with him instead of Leah. Surely even that wasn't too hard for *Der Herr*.

Instead, Jacob had heard these words. Ones he'd read over and over again. *Be still, and know that I am God. My thoughts are not your thoughts neither are your ways my ways, saith the Lord.* Those and, *Trust in the Lord with all thine heart and lean not unto thine own understanding.*

The words hadn't been what Jacob had wanted to hear, but they humbled him. He wasn't God. God's ways were perfect, his were not. All he *could* do was trust.

Either that or do things his own way. That had never worked out well in the past. It likely wouldn't now either.

The *ferhoodled* thoughts in his head told him to escape the Amish with Rachel—now that she was of legal marrying age, divorce Leah, and leave his *boppli* fatherless. But he couldn't and wouldn't do anything of the sort. *Ach*, the devil would surely rejoice if Jacob succumbed to a ridiculous scheme like that. He had to keep his head.

Nee, he did care for his *fraa* and *boppli*. He wasn't about to give them up. But he didn't want to lose his beloved either.

"Help me to trust You, *Gott*. Because I can't do this on my own. You know how much I love Rachel. I don't understand Your ways. Somehow, *Gott*, make this all work out."

TWENTY-EIGHT

*J*acob strummed his fingers on his pant legs. He was ready for Sunday meeting to be over with and it hadn't even begun yet. Not the best attitude to have, especially on *Der Herr's* day.

"Rumor has it that Rachel's back on the market," the young man next to him whispered.

Jacob frowned. He didn't even want to acknowledge Jeriah's comment.

"So, does that mean she's free? Like totally? Because if she is, I'd really like to court her."

Jacob grunted.

"Are you okay with that? I mean, I know the two of you dated for a long time and planned to marry." He shrugged. "But you're married to Leah now, so…"

"Rachel can do whatever she wants. She doesn't need my permission." Anger simmered beneath his words. *Nee*, not anger. Hurt. Devastation. Sorrow.

Jeriah sighed contently. "Good. Because I plan to ask her to ride home with me tonight. *Ach*, she's *sehr schee*."

Jacob shot up from the bench and raced outside. *Ach*, he couldn't spend another moment in that stifling house. He'd miss meeting, and he'd likely be reprimanded for it. But he couldn't sit there and just pretend that everything was okay.

Everything was *not* okay. Not even close. He had wed Leah for Rachel. He was producing *bopplin* for Rachel. He would eventually become a widower for Rachel. Rachel was his life. His breath.

The thought of losing her for good to another man was more than he could take.

Why had he ever agreed to Marlin's *ferhoodled* plan in the first place? How had he thought this would ever work out?

But Jacob knew. He'd had faith in his and Rachel's love. That it was strong enough to weather any storm. That it could withstand anything.

Now, he wasn't so sure.

Rachel had given up on them. And that wounded him more than any sword piercing his flesh ever would. *Ach*, his heart was surely bleeding.

He wanted to beg her. To fall at her feet and plea for a stay of execution. Wasn't love loyal? Didn't love suffer long? Hope all things? Believe all things? Endure all things? Didn't she have faith in their love?

He needed to talk to her again. Reason with her. Convince her to change her mind.

○∽

"Where are you going?" Leah called to Jacob just as he placed his hat on his head, ready to escape the house and scurry outside.

"Out. I have something to do." He grumbled.

"Now? On *Der Herr's* day?" Her disapproval was evident.

"*Jah.*"

"Jacob, whatever it is, you can talk to me about it." She was likely concerned about his departure from church this morning, although she hadn't brought it up, to her credit.

"*Nee.* I can't."

"Is it Rachel?"

He opened the door. "I have to go. Don't wait up for me."

"Jacob…"

He stepped outside before he heard all her words. He didn't have time for a conversation right now. He needed to get back to the Millers' place, where they'd be having the young folks' gathering tonight. He had to stop Rachel before she made a terrible mistake and ruined everything.

჻

Although Jacob wasn't much older than the young folks present, he felt like a chaperone rather than one of the attendees. Especially with his beard.

Ach, it seemed like forever since he'd been to one of these gatherings. How many times had he escorted Rachel home from a singing?

As a matter of fact, she'd been the only *maedel* he'd taken home in this district. Since they'd fallen madly in love, he never had a reason to take anyone else home.

Perhaps tonight, he could rekindle that flame. Make Rachel remember the reason she'd chosen him in the first place.

Rachel must have seen him pull up, because she met him at the door. "Jacob, what are you doing here?"

"I've come to take you home." He couldn't help but smile.

She took his arm and maneuvered him outside. No doubt to be away from eavesdropping ears. "*Nee,*

Jacob. I'm not riding home with you. Go home to Leah and your *boppli*."

"I don't want Leah. I never wanted Leah. I want you. It's always been you." He lifted a hand to her cheek.

She stepped back. "It's too late, Jacob."

"*Nee*, it's not. My heart belongs to you, Rachel."

"But, don't you see? It shouldn't. Your heart should reside with your *fraa*."

"You are my future *fraa*. The *only* reason I'm married to Leah now."

"Things have changed, Jacob."

"What? What has changed? Can you honestly say that you don't love me anymore?"

"*Ach*, Jacob, you know I'll always love you."

"I fail to see the problem. You love me. I love you. We want to marry and we will. Eventually."

"Jacob, please. Don't make this any harder than it is. We've already had this conversation. I gave you my reasons. You need to accept that."

"Why?"

She stepped close and placed a kiss on his cheek. "Goodbye, Jacob. Enjoy your family. Have a nice life."

Have a nice...? He stood, watching her walk away, just like he had the other night. But for some reason, this time felt final. It felt real.

Like this was it.

Like she no longer believed in them.

Like she was never coming back.

Marlin approached Jacob the next morning as they worked on the farm chores.

"Rachel says you showed up at the singing last night to take her home."

"*Jah*, I did."

"You should not be taking *maed* home when you have a *fraa* and *boppli* at home. You are dishonoring the *familye Der Herr* has given you."

"*Der Herr? Der Herr* has nothing to do with this, Marlin! You're the one who got me into this whole mess in the first place. You forced Leah and me together when you *knew* I wanted to marry Rachel. I loved Rachel. I still do." He began walking away. Because it was better that he didn't let his simmering emotions show.

"Let her be, Jacob."

He spun around, took two steps, and grasped a fistful of Marlin's shirt collar. "Don't you dare tell me what to do ever again. You've ruined my life!"

He needed to walk away before he did something

else he'd regret. He was in no condition to be around anybody. *Nee*, at this point, he didn't even want to be around himself.

TWENTY-NINE

The following year...

Jacob had waited for *Der Herr* to do something. To step in. To intervene. To stop the wedding plans.

He'd waited. And waited. And waited. It hadn't happened. Nothing had happened.

Well, nothing except the forward progress of Rachel's wedding to Jeriah.

He could not abide the thought of Rachel being married off. At least, if she remained single, they'd eventually be able to wed. But if she married Jeriah, a wedding between the two of them would never take place. All his hopes and dreams would die.

She'd been promised to him on the condition he married Leah and fathered *bopplin*. Well, he'd done his part. He'd been waiting patiently. He would continue to wait patiently. He would *not* let Rachel be stolen away. Not even by a *gut* Amish man like his cousin Jeriah.

He wasn't exactly sure what he'd do. But he'd think of something. He had to.

Rachel's hands trembled as she fastened the front of her royal blue cape dress. Had she really agreed to marry Jeriah? He was handsome enough. Kind enough. But he wasn't her beloved Jacob.

It would be a miracle if she could get through this day. Especially without breaking down in tears. Because, in reality, this was the death of a dream.

A knock sounded on the other side of the door. *Ach*, it was almost time.

You can do this. You can do this. She'd been trying to convince herself all morning, but now that it was almost here, she was having serious doubts.

She still needed to don her crisp white apron, but otherwise she was fully dressed. She guessed it to be one of her side sitters.

"*Kumm* in."

The door opened and Jacob walked in. He swiftly locked the door behind him.

She gasped. *Ach*, but he was bold! And ever so handsome. She practically melted like a puddle of simmering dark chocolate right in front of him.

"Jacob. What are you doing here?" She remembered Jacob and Leah's wedding. She'd had no desire to attend. *Nee*, she'd wanted to be as far away as possible. The thought of watching her beloved wed another had been unbearable.

Jacob took her hands in his. "Rachel, I will do *anything* to prevent you from marrying Jeriah. Please don't." His tone was desperate.

"Jacob…" The hopelessness in his eyes ripped at her heart.

"*Kumm*, let's go away. Just you and me."

Her heart sped up at his words. If only…

"We can leave right now. I will divorce Leah and we can marry in the *Englisch* world." His eyes searched hers.

He was serious. She closed her eyes and considered what he'd said. *He was serious?*

"You would divorce Leah and abandon your *bopplin*…for me?" The very thought was tragic. "*Nee*, you cannot do that. Leah would be devastated."

"*Please*, Rachel, I can't lose you! I don't know what else I can do!" Tears ran down his cheeks. "Rachel, it was all for you. If you—"

She held up a hand to stop him. "Jacob, I know you love me. Probably more than any person should love another human being. And I love you too. But leaving would only complicate matters."

"Don't you see, Rachel? *Nothing* else matters to me as much as you. Nothing."

She sighed. "Okay, I won't marry Jeriah. But I also will not let you leave Leah and your *bopplin*. *Ach*, Jacob. How can you even consider leaving those precious little *buwe*? And my sister's in no condition to raise them on her own."

"I didn't want to. But when faced with the prospect of losing the woman I love more than life itself, there is no sacrifice too great."

"But it would be wrong. *Der Herr* would not be pleased."

"Rachel, our whole situation has been wrong from the day your *vatter* interfered and insisted I marry your *schweschder*. It would serve him right."

"Maybe. But don't you see? Innocent people would get hurt. They would suffer even more than they already are." *Ach*, Jacob had not been thinking straight. He was making decisions based on emotion instead of thinking through the consequences.

"I will wait for you, Jacob. I promise. Even if it takes decades." *Ach*, but she hoped it didn't. Yet, hoping that it didn't caused her to feel guilty. Because their marriage would only happen after her sister's passing. And, even as much as she and Leah quarreled, she would never wish her sister dead. Never. Nor would she wish her divorced and a single mother.

"Really? For real? You really will?" He sounded like a child who'd been promised a stick of candy from the store.

At her nod, he brought her close and clutched her to his chest. *Ach*, it felt so so good to be in Jacob's arms. *Jah*, she'd wait for him. Even if it took years. Because one day as Jacob's *fraa* would surely be better than a ten thousand as someone else's.

"*Ach*, I don't ever want to let you go." A heavy sigh escaped Jacob's lips. *Jah*, she felt the same way.

But someone needed to announce that the wedding wouldn't take place. She dreaded the look on poor Jeriah's face. But she didn't love him. She'd been deceiving herself to think a marriage between the two of them could work. He'd be better off without her. Jacob would always be her one and only.

"Will you…will you ask Jeriah to come here?" She would try to sound strong for Jeriah's sake.

He nodded. "*Jah*. I will. I'll also tell the bishop the wedding's off. No doubt, he'll want to counsel with you." He eyed her.

"I will tell him that I can't marry Jeriah. That I've decided to wait for you. Surely the visitors can still enjoy a nice meal, *jah*?"

His brow arched. "*Jah*. But without the joy of a bride and groom, it might be awkward."

He squeezed her hand for support. She read the relief, the thankfulness in his eyes. "Okay, I'll fetch Jeriah now."

Rachel sent up a quick prayer the moment Jacob walked out. Hopefully, Jeriah would be understanding.

The door opened then shut.

Jeriah's smile stretched wide across his face as he walked in. He stepped close and took her hands in his. "You ready to get hitched?" *Ach*, she heard the excitement in his voice. His eyes alight with joy. This was no doubt the most exciting day of his life.

She swallowed. *Ach*, she didn't want to hurt him. She forced herself to look into his eyes. She at least owed him that much. "I...I can't, Jeriah. I'm sorry." Tears naturally came at the words.

His smile was exchanged for a frown. "What do you mean?" He shook his head. "*Nee*, Rachel. This is it. This is our day."

"I still love Jacob. I can't marry you."

"*Ach, lieb*. I know that. But Jacob's married with

kinner. You'll eventually get over him. Once we start a family togeth—"

"*Nee*, I'm going to wait for Jacob." Her hands trembled.

"Rachel, don't be *narrisch*. Will you wait until you're an old woman?"

"If I have to."

"*Nee*, Rachel. Please, *lieb*, don't do this. I…I love you."

"But I don't love you. My heart belongs to Jacob. It always will." Her chest heaved. "*Ach*, Jeriah. Don't you see? You'll be better off with somebody else. Someone who deserves your love. Someone who will give you her whole heart. That's not me."

He sighed. "But everyone is here. Our family. Our friends. If you were going to change your mind, I wish you'd done it sooner. I've already spent so much money and… What am I going to say to everyone? I'll look like a fool."

She shook her head and cupped his cheek with her hand. "You are not a fool, Jeriah. You are a *gut* man. Any *maedel* will be blessed to have you as an *ehemann*."

"Just not you." He swallowed.

"Even me. But I can't marry you when my heart belongs to someone else. I just can't. I'm sorry, Jeriah."

"Not as sorry as I am."

"You will find someone." She lifted a teasing smile. "I've heard Betty Yoder has had her eye on you."

"*Ach*, really?" His face lit up. "I guess she's almost as pretty as you."

"*Nee*, she's prettier. And she's really sweet, too."

"*Jah*, I guess she is." He shrugged.

"Maybe she'll let you take her home tonight after the supper."

"*Ach, nee*. It's too soon. It will take me longer than that to get over you, Rachel Schmidt. I'm being brave in front of you." His hand covered his heart.

"*Jah, vell*, don't wait too long. I hear she's a fine catch."

He laughed and shook his head. His grin brought a smile to her own face.

"I'll miss you, Rachel." He bent down and kissed her cheek. "I hope you and Jacob…" He shrugged. "Well, you know." He raised a small smile, took two steps and exited the room.

She couldn't help her feelings—a mixture of sadness and relief. And thankfulness that Jeriah took it so well. "*Gott*, please be with Jeriah and heal his heart. Help him to find another *maedel* quickly. And help me to be patient while waiting for Jacob, my beloved."

THIRTY

Ten years later…

Rachel knew the time was getting close. She'd been attending to Leah and her *kinner* for the past few years, helping with household chores and caring for each new *boppli* that entered the King home.

Jacob's growing family had since switched dwelling places with Rachel and her father to accommodate their rapidly expanding tribe. Rachel didn't mind the *dawdi haus* but it seemed like she was in Jacob and Leah's home more often than not. Many times, she'd slept on their couch, to be able to tend to the needs of the *kinner* when their folks could not.

But now, with every day that passed, Rachel's sister grew weaker, frailer.

"*Aenti* Rachel, will you play *haus* with me and my *bopplin*?" Young Dinah, the only *maedel* of Jacob and Leah's nine *kinner,* held up a faceless doll.

"*Jah*, in just a minute. I need to take this tea to your *mamm*," she said to her five-year-old niece.

"Will you bring out baby Zeb so he can play with us too?"

"*Nee*, *liebling*. The *boppli's* sleeping with your *mamm* right now." Rachel smiled. *Ach*, Jacob's *kinner* were precious.

She carried the teacup and saucer—a set she'd recognized from Leah's dower chest—to the bedroom. She came near and sat on the bed. Leah's eyes were closed, but Rachel guessed she was only resting and not asleep. She'd been doing a lot of that lately.

"Here, sister, drink."

"*Nee*." Leah pushed the cup away with her limp hand.

"The *dochter* said it is *gut* for you. It will help you feel better," she insisted.

"Don't want it." Leah took Rachel's hand. Her hand felt cool to the touch.

Rachel set the cup on the nightstand near the bed. "Not feeling *gut* today?" She attempted to keep the worry out of her tone.

"*Nee*, Rachel." She heaved a slow labored breath. "Love Jacob and the *bopplin*. Be a *gut fraa* to Jacob and *mamm* to my *kinner*."

Tears pricked Rachel's eyes. "*Ach*, Leah. I will. I

promise. But you are not leaving us yet." She said the words, trying to believe they were true. She doubted they were though.

"I…need…rest…" Leah closed her heavy eyelids.

Rachel began to panic. *Nee*, her *schweschder* couldn't be… She watched Leah closely until she noticed that her chest continued to rise and fall. She sighed in relief.

She didn't have much longer, but Rachel wasn't ready to lose her sister yet. Thirty-six years was hardly a full life. But at least she had known the love of a husband, and the blessing of being a *mamm*. The latter was something Rachel might never know firsthand, no matter how many years *Der Herr* blessed her with on earth.

Confident Leah was still alive, she took the tea back to the kitchen. It was time to play *haus* with sweet Dinah.

Jacob walked into the house with his six oldest boys in tow. "Wash up. Reuben, Judah, help the younger *buwe*. It smells like supper might be ready soon."

The boys cheered simultaneously.

Jacob chuckled, removed his boots, and washed his own hands. No better way to a boy's heart than through his stomach.

"I wonder what *Aenti* Rachel made for us tonight." He caught her eye, as she stirred a pot of something on the stove, and lifted a half-smile.

Her return smile was wobbly. *Ach*, it must've been a hard day. He walked into the kitchen. He rested his hands on her shoulders, then examined her face and stared intently into her eyes. "You doing okay?"

She gave a slight nod, but tears pooled in her eyes. "We're losing her, Jacob." She spoke in a whisper, likely so the *kinner* wouldn't overhear.

He swallowed and frowned. "I know."

She shook her head. "I'm...I'm not ready yet."

"I know. Neither am I. But when the time comes, *Der Herr* will give us the strength to get through it."

He wanted to pull her into his arms, but they'd agreed to very limited physical contact once Rachel had begun helping out with the *kinner* and staying overnight in the house. No need to fuel the fires of temptation.

"I will need *you* too, Jacob."

"I will be here for you. You can count on that." He nodded. "I'm going to check on my *fraa* before supper."

"*Jah*, that is a *gut* idea."

"Did she eat anything today?"

"Not much."

"How were the other *kinner*?"

"They were *gut*. Dinah and I had a tea party today."

That brought a smile to her face.

"I bet that was fun."

"It was."

He hurried out of the room, anxious to see his *fraa*.

Jacob abruptly stopped at the door of the bedroom and stood, staring at his wife. Leah lay in their bed. It was the same bed each of their *bopplin* had been created in—the beginning of life. But now…now… He swallowed. She seemed so frail, so helpless.

Ach, his *fraa* was dying. Jacob closed his burning eyes and fought back the volley of tears. He hadn't expected to feel this much emotion for Leah, the *fraa* thrust upon him by his father-in-law. But, because he'd desired to be the husband *Gott* had called him to be, he'd learned to love her. *Nee*, he hadn't been the perfect *ehemann* by any means, but he'd tried.

And, in spite of the fact that her death would mean he and Rachel could finally marry, he didn't want to let Leah go. He wasn't ready. He didn't want to lose her. *Jah*, he'd assured Rachel that *Der Herr* would help them through it, but now he questioned whether he could *ever* get over the passing of the mother of his *kinner*.

What would he tell the *kinner*? How would they get through such a tragedy? Would they even accept *Aenti* Rachel as their new *mamm*?

He crawled into bed next to his *fraa* and held her close. She barely responded. He kissed the top of her head, allowing his tears to flow freely. *Ach*, this was so hard!

"*Ich liebe dich*, Leah." He reached for her hand, brought it to his lips, then held it close to his heart. He felt a faint squeeze in response. She knew he was there.

He rubbed her hand lightly with his thumb. "Don't worry, *lieb*. I will be here for you. The *kinner* will be taken care of."

Reuben, their oldest son, stopped at the door's opening. His eyes slightly widened as he took in the scene in front of him. "*Dat*, *Aenti* Rachel says supper is ready and on the table."

He nodded. "Tell her I'm going to stay here with your *mamm*. You all may go ahead and eat without me. Save me some." He attempted to muster a smile, but it refused to materialize.

"Okay, *Dat*." Reuben glanced at his *mamm*, his chin quivering momentarily, then flew from the room.

Ach, Gott, help us through this.

Rachel slowly walked into the bedroom after the children had all eaten, a bowl of warm soup in hand. She'd made soft homemade chicken noodles this evening hoping that Leah might take some nourishment.

"I brought soup. I thought Leah might—" She glanced up at Jacob. His eyes were red-rimmed and tears soaked his beard as he held Leah in his arms. Her heart tripped. "Jacob?"

"She…she's gone."

THIRTY-ONE

The days and weeks following Leah's funeral had been some of the toughest in both Jacob's and Rachel's lives. Rachel had washed and prepared her sister's body for burial, as she and Leah had prepared their *mamm's* fifteen years prior. Death was never easy, but it was an unavoidable part of life.

"It was *Der Herr's* will," the bishop had said at the funeral.

But Rachel questioned whether it really was *Der Herr's* will. If *Gott* originally created man to live forever and if He was not willing that any should perish, then how could it be *Gott's* will? He had allowed it, *jah*, but that didn't mean He willed it, ain't not?

Perhaps she would ask Jacob about it. He seemed to know much more about the Bible and the ways of *Der Herr* than she did.

Since Rachel had become somewhat of a permanent fixture in the lives of the *kinner* and in Jacob's household, the leaders agreed that a marriage ceremony held sooner rather than later would be best for propriety's sake. So their nuptials had been planned one month after Leah's passing, as opposed to the usual waiting period. She was quite certain her *vatter* held some sway in that decision.

Jacob sent invitations to his family in Kentucky. His *mamm* responded with a letter informing him that his father had become ill and they wouldn't be able to make the trip. She invited him to come back home and bring his family. She'd included a generous financial gift as well for their wedding present.

They hadn't heard back from his *bruder* Ephraim. Rachel worried that he might still harbor ill feelings toward Jacob. If he still sought revenge, then there was no way she'd agree to moving to Kentucky, as Jacob had mentioned.

A houseful of *kinner* made quiet time alone challenging. Rachel and Jacob had to wait until the children went to bed and the littlest one was satisfied before they could spend time together. Because they both carried physically demanding work schedules, they often fell asleep while talking on the couch, usually with Rachel nestled in Jacob's strong arms.

Jacob would wake up in the middle of the night, cover Rachel with a blanket, and find his way to his bedroom. It wouldn't be acceptable for the *kinner* to find them asleep together in the morning, even if it was on the sofa.

Since the *boppli* had only been a couple months old when Leah passed on, he still needed nourishment fairly often. Rachel would fix his bottles of diluted goatmilk and warm them as needed. It seemed to prove a suitable substitute for the breast milk he'd missed out on.

While Leah was alive, Rachel had always been a little envious of her sister when it came to nursing. Knowing she'd likely never have her own *bopplin,* if the doctor was correct, had been difficult to accept. But at least she'd still been blessed with the opportunity to hold Jacob's little ones in her arms, to be a substitute *mamm* for them.

Rachel persuaded Jacob to call his *mamm* and ask about Ephraim. Her words had been encouraging, but they lacked the assurance Rachel had been hoping for. She'd simply said that Ephraim had moved away and the last time Jacob had come up in conversation, his brother didn't grunt or spew out hatred.

That was a *gut* thing, *jah*, but to Rachel's thinking, that didn't mean it was safe for Jacob to return home.

It would be wonderful *gut* if the two brothers could iron out their differences. Jacob's *mamm* seemed confident that scenario could actually happen. Rachel still wasn't sure.

THIRTY-TWO

Rachel could scarcely believe her day had finally arrived. It was today. Today. Today—*this* day!—she would marry—marry!—Jacob King, the man she'd been dreaming about for entirely too long. *Ach*, she didn't think she could love him any more than she did now. It seemed like every day he would say or do something that would make her heart swell with love for him. She might just burst with joy before the day was over.

Ach, Jacob.

A hundred funerals couldn't wipe the smile off her face. Okay, maybe a *hundred* could. But she was happy. Happy. Thrilled. Exhilarated. Ecstatic. She would cherish every single second of this day. Instill it in her memory. Engrave it on her heart. Etch it on her soul.

This was truly the best day ever!

Jacob grasped the hand of his bride as they stood before the bishop and congregation of friends and loved ones. *Ach*, Rachel, his beloved, would finally be his. At long last.

Words could not express how much he loved this woman. Her care of his *kinner* and Leah during her last days had only intensified his love for her.

The years did nothing to diminish her beauty. *Nee*, they only magnified it. Her facial features had become more defined. And her curves, well…

He swallowed. *Ach…jah.*

He wouldn't let his mind go there right now. He forced himself to refocus his thoughts.

He and Leah had gotten along fine. He was thankful for the time they'd had together, in spite of Marlin's coercion. And he would certainly miss her. They'd had a pretty *gut* marriage. They'd been pretty *gut* parents. They were even pretty *gut* lovers.

But Rachel…

Ach, he'd loved her for so long. Just the thought of taking her in his arms and claiming his first real kiss as his *fraa* sent his heart cartwheeling.

He wondered what Rachel would think of the surprises he'd planned. Her cousins should be at the house right now implementing the changes he'd requested. Rearranging the bedroom furniture. Putting away Leah's quilt and dishes—he'd store those away for Dinah. Replacing them with the colorful new ones he'd purchased for Rachel as a wedding gift. And sprucing up their home with new curtains. He hoped she'd be pleased.

One thing he'd learned while being married to Leah was that when he blessed others by showing selfless acts of kindness, he himself would be blessed in return.

Before he even realized it, the ceremony ended and they were being carted off to their *Eck*. Rachel's eyes sparkled with love and what appeared to be adoration. *Ach*, he adored this woman—now his *fraa*.

He nearly jumped when she reached her hand under the table and squeezed his thigh. *Ach*. He promptly redirected her hand by intertwining her fingers with his. They'd have to wait until they returned home for…other things.

He didn't miss Rachel's teasing smile. *Jah*, he'd chosen his *fraa* wisely for sure and certain.

THIRTY-THREE

Rachel had fun flirting with Jacob during their wedding reception, but now that they were home and the *kinner* were asleep in their beds...

Nee, she wouldn't be nervous. Just because Jacob had way more experience...*nee,* not way *more* because she had none.

Nevertheless, she was certain their wedding night would be *wunderbaar* indeed.

"*Kumm*, my beloved, *mei fraa*. In the words of Solomon, *let us take our fill of love till morning*." He held out his hand and pulled her close to him.

Ach. Surely she must have turned twenty shades of pink as his hands deftly pulled out the pins in her *kapp* and hair.

His lips teased hers momentarily before he moved to her jaw, down her neck.

Perhaps they should relocate from the kitchen to

their bedroom in case one of the *kinner* awoke. "Jacob?"

"*Jah*?" He breathed out, not even stopping his forward progress.

"We should…"

He removed the pins of her apron.

"*Ach*…the bedroom?" She whimpered.

"*Jah*." He promptly whisked her up into his arms and strode to their love nest. He gently set her down beside the bed. A beautifully covered bed with a quilt she'd never seen. Where had it come from?

"Now, where were we?" His lips found hers again, but with unrestricted passion this time.

Warmth spread through her entire being when he drew her as close as their clothing allowed. She unfastened his vest and pushed his suspenders off his shoulders. She moved to his shirt buttons.

He began removing the pins from her dress.

A wail resounded from the other room.

"*Ach*, it's Zeb." She moved back.

"*Nee*." He brought her close again, delighting in his husbandly privileges.

The wail sounded louder.

"Just…he can wait a little bit." Jacob insisted, quickly removing his shirt.

Instead of focusing on her *ehemann's* well-defined

chest, she was distracted by the *boppli*.

"*Dat, Aenti* Rachel," a small voice called.

Their attention snapped to the door. *Ach*, in their haste they'd forgotten to close it. Five wide-eyed *kinner* stood in the doorway.

Rachel quickly covered herself, though she was still mostly fully clothed.

"*Ach, nee*." Jacob grimaced. "What are you doing awake?"

"The *boppli* kept crying," Judah complained.

"Well, why didn't one of you pick him up? You know how to change a diaper and feed him." Jacob frowned.

"*Aenti* Rachel always does it," Reuben reminded.

"One of you can do it tonight," Jacob insisted. "Now close the door, take care of the *boppli*, and go get back in bed."

"What were you doing?" Levi's wide eyes moved from Jacob to Rachel. "Teacher Leah, *Mamm*, always said not to touch the girls."

Jacob gritted his teeth. "You can when you're married to them. Now get to bed." He promptly shut the door himself.

He moved back to the bed. "Now, where were we?"

Rachel couldn't help it. She burst into laughter. After a split-second, Jacob joined in and they laughed until tears ran down their cheeks.

"*Ach*, we must be the only ones who have had a wedding night like this." Rachel said through her tears.

"*Jah*, for sure." He chuckled.

He put his hand to her cheek, attempting to find some semblance of gravity after their interruption. He tried to force the side of his mouth down, to no avail. "Now, where were we?"

They both exploded into laughter again, unable to contain their mirth.

sheep. They had been a labor of love, not to mention her companions. And although Jacob primarily cared for them now, anytime Rachel was near, the creatures would be at her beck and call.

The money *Mamm* had sent would help immensely with their relocation and traveling costs. They'd need to hire a couple of cattle trailers to transport the creatures to their new home state.

"Marlin, I need to speak with you."

Marlin looked up from the low stool he'd been milking from. "Say on."

He folded his hands together. "I'm taking Rachel and the *kinner*. We're moving back to my home state, Kentucky."

Marlin grunted.

Jacob stood there, waiting for some kind of reply. He waited in vain. Perhaps Marlin needed some time to mull over the news he'd just delivered.

Marlin finally glanced up. "You gonna finish your work or not?"

"Uh, *jah*." He swallowed. "Well, uh, we'll begin packing soon. We plan to head out next week. That will give you a little time to find someone." He shrugged. "If you want to hire help."

Ach, Jacob hadn't really thought about how much Marlin would be losing. Not only his family and free help around the farm, but his cook, his laundress, his housekeeper. They'd be leaving him in the lurch for sure.

Be that as it may, there wasn't much he could do about it. He wouldn't forfeit precious time with his folks to stay here longer with Marlin. He'd already given him several years of his life—after being beguiled. He refused to sacrifice any more of his family's life on his father-in-law's behalf.

Marlin sighed. "I don't want you to go."

"I know. But we need to. It's time. I need to establish my own household."

"And you have a home for my *kinskinner*?"

"I do. My *vatter* and *Grossdawdi* built a nice log cabin."

Marlin sneered. "You wish to raise my *kinskinner* in a cabin?"

"It's plenty large. Lots of property too. They will like it."

"But they won't know anyone there. You'll be uprooting them from the only place they've ever known. Taking them away from memories of their *mudder*."

"I think the older ones will always remember her no matter where we go. The little ones may not remember her at all. But Rachel is their *mamm* now. She's already been caring for them for quite some time. The little ones consider her their *mamm*."

"Do not forget my Leah." His voice seemed husky to Jacob's ears. Was Marlin getting emotional?

"*Nee*, I'll never forget her. She was my first *fraa* and the mother of my *bopplin*. She will not be forgotten." He shifted from foot to foot, pushing a clod of dirt around with the toe of his boot. "Look, Marlin. We *are* going to go. But we will not cut you out of our lives. We will write to you. And you will always be welcome to come visit us in Kentucky."

His father-in-law nodded.

"We'll be taking Rachel's sheep along as well. And some of the herd."

"*Nee*, you won't."

"I will. I'll consider it my pay for working for you all these years. You don't need them. Besides, I'm leaving you plenty. Look how much I've increased your livestock, Marlin. You can sell off the extra, if you want, and make a nice living."

"But I can see the hand of *Der Herr* is with you. If you leave, He might stop blessing me."

"*Ach*, Marlin. It's true that I am a blessed man. I would never deny that. But *Gott's* blessings aren't exclusive to me. Repent of your sins and serve *Der Herr* with your whole heart and He will bless you."

He grabbed a pitchfork to muck out one of the stalls. They worked in companionable silence until one of the *kinner* called them in for breakfast.

Jacob had expected resistance, but that conversation had gone better than he'd hoped for. Surely *Der Herr* was blessing his every step.

THIRTY-FIVE

Rachel's heart soared when their hired van finally arrived to embark on their journey. *Ach*, ever since Jacob mentioned his folks, she felt like she'd instantly fallen in love with them. If they were anything like their son—and she figured they were—they would be *wunderbaar grosseldern* for their *kinner*.

The trip would be long, especially traveling with the *kinner*, but at least they'd only have one overnight stay in a motel. If it was only her and Jacob, a motel stay would have sounded like fun, but with all the *kinner*, not so much. *Nee*, the sooner they arrived at their destination, the better.

The men with the cattle trailers had arrived yesterday and took her precious sheep with them. She was thankful that Jacob wanted to bring them along. Although she was busy with the *kinner* for the most part, sheering season and wool collection and processing happened only once a year for a short period of time. Some of the *kinner* were old enough to help out, either with minding the *bopplin* or with washing the wool.

Jacob strolled up behind her and snaked his arms around her waist, nuzzling her neck as she stared out the window daydreaming. "You ready to go, *schatzi*?"

"*Jah*, I'm ready. I think." She went through the mental list of items they'd need to have handy in the van. "Does the driver know he'll probably have to stop often so the *kinner* can use the bathroom?"

"*Jah*. Maybe we should have hired someone with a motorhome. *Ach*, I wish I would have thought of that sooner."

"That would be much easier, I think. But I'm sure it'll be fine."

"Did you pack extra changes of clothes for the trip in case someone has an accident?"

She nodded. "Clothes, diaper bag, snacks, blankets, pillows...I hope I didn't forget anything."

"If it's something we need, we can always stop at a store and buy it."

"*Jah*. Okay. That makes me feel better." She turned in his arms and indulged in a kiss.

"You ready to say goodbye to your *vatter*?"

"I think so." She sighed. Her *dat* had been trying her

patience the last few days. At every turn, he'd tried to talk her into staying there with him. When had her *vatter* become so needy?

"Don't worry about him. He'll be fine."

"You think so? We're the closest family he has. I feel like I'm abandoning him."

"Can you keep a secret?" Jacob's brow shot up.

Rachel pulled back and stared at him. "What?"

"Your *vatter* has an *aldi*."

She playfully slapped his upper arm. "*Ach*, he does not!"

"Mm...hm." He nodded.

"Who?"

"Margaret Yoder."

"The *alt maedel*? She's like at least ten years younger than *Dat*! *Ach*, really?"

He held up two fingers. "I lie not."

"How do you know?"

"Saw them at the hardware store. They didn't think anyone was around. When he handed her the money from across the counter, their hands lingered a little too long. But it was the look in her eye and smile that gave it away. *Jah*, they're sweet on each other for sure."

"*Ach*, I never would have thought!"

"They kind of make a nice couple, ain't so?"

She shrugged. "Can't see her being my *mamm*."

The door opened and Marlin waltzed in. *Ach*, did he seem joyful? Perhaps Jacob was right. Perhaps he'd just been waiting for the right time to take another *fraa*. "You two gonna stand there smoochin' all day? That driver's been waiting. Said the *kinner* are all buckled in now."

"*Jah*." Jacob pulled *Dat* in for a hug.

"*Der Herr* go with you, *sohn*."

Jacob nodded. "And may He be with you too."

Rachel stepped close and wrapped her father in an embrace. "I'll miss you, *Dat*."

"I'll miss you too, *dochder*." He pulled back with unshed tears in his eyes. "Don't you worry about me."

"Okay." She shook her finger in his direction. "We'll expect you to visit with your new *fraa*."

His eyes nearly jumped out of their sockets.

"You don't fool me." She winked, spun around, and headed toward the awaiting vehicle, leaving her father with his chin on the ground.

THIRTY-SIX

"*Y*ou *buwe* will like *Grossdawdi's* ranch. He has a lot of horses." Jacob turned from his seat and looked back at the older boys in the seat behind him, Rachel, and the *boppli*. "Nice ones that run on the racetrack and sell for a lot of money."

That brightened the boys' gloomy faces. "Really?"

Jah, they'd been traveling too long. Thankfully, they were almost home. *Home! Ach*, he couldn't wait to see *Mamm* and *Dat*. He was sure they'd love his tribe.

"*Jah*, and Dinah, your *Grossmammi* will teach you how to make goat milk soap."

Dinah smiled. "She will?"

"*Ach*, I can't wait to learn." Rachel squeezed his hand.

"Almost there," the driver called out. "Is everyone ready to stretch their legs?"

A collective *'jah'* echoed back.

The driver pulled around the corner. Jacob squinted to see in the distance. *Ach*, was it Ephraim? And he appeared to have a large group of men with him, both Amish and *Englisch*. They looked rough enough to turn a city upside down. They blocked the entrance to the driveway.

Jacob gulped. This might not go well. *Gott, please be with me*.

He turned to Rachel. "My brother's here. I want you and the *kinner* to stay in the van until I call you to come out. Okay?"

He'd speak with the driver to make sure he stayed with Rachel and the *kinner*. If any foul play ensued, he'd be directed to leave at once. Because if Ephraim had in mind to finish him off, he would not harm his *fraa* and *kinner*.

She looked to where his gaze had been, then glanced back at him. He read the worry in her eyes.

"It'll be okay, *lieb. Der Herr* will go with me." *Ach*, he wished he felt the confidence his words exuded.

The vehicle stopped.

Jacob inhaled a deep breath and sent up another prayer. He leaned over and kissed Rachel on the cheek. "I'll be right back." He smiled to reassure her.

He briefly spoke with his driver, then walked toward

the large group of men. Like he was walking the plank of a ship. Or stepping up to the gallows. Or—

"Jacob, *bruder*! Is that you?" Ephraim careened toward him at full speed, practically knocking him off his feet with a huge bear hug. "I hardly recognize you with that beard. That's mighty impressive."

"You…you're not…*ach*, I brought some cattle. It should have arrived yesterday. I brought some for you."

Ephraim waved a hand in front of his face. "*Ach*, I don't need it. I've got tons."

"I insist."

"Jacob, you don't need to butter me up. We're good." Ephraim stared him in the eye. "I don't harbor any ill will toward you."

His eyes widened. "You don't? You've forgiven me?"

"*Jah*. Will you forgive me for being such a jerk?"

Ach…

Denki, Gott!

"*Jah*."

Ephraim turned back and waved the men behind him over.

Jacob blew out a breath. Hopefully, Ephraim was serious. Because, if he wasn't…

"Hey, guys! Come meet my baby brother!" Ephraim called out.

The men came over and shook his hand. Amazement filled Jacob. *Ach*, he did not deserve *Gott's* goodness!

"Hey, he's only older by a minute," Jacob teased.

"I will claim whatever victory I can get, *bruder*." Ephraim slapped him on the back.

Jacob turned and signaled to the driver.

"Who do you have with you?" Ephraim peered over Jacob's shoulder.

"*Mei fraa und kinner*."

Rachel's contented smile warmed him as she approached, holding the *boppli* in her arms. Dinah held the second youngest's hand. And the boys trailed behind them.

Jacob slipped his arm around Rachel's waist. "This is my *fraa*, Rachel. And our *kinner*."

Ephraim's expression widened. "Wow, you have nine already? You're a stud."

Jacob coughed. His *bruder* had been in the *Englisch* world too long. Jacob shook his head and gently squeezed his *fraa*. He hoped Ephraim's careless words didn't harm Rachel.

"*Der Herr* has blessed us." Jacob wouldn't explain that the *kinner* were from his first marriage. Rachel was their *mamm* now.

"How about you? *Fraa*? *Kinner*?" He'd already known the answers due to *Mamm's* letters, but he wanted to keep the conversation going.

"Two kids. My wife's *Englisch*. We've got a decent place."

"We'd like to meet them someday." He smiled.

"Sure. We'll stop by one of these days." He glanced at the children. "Well, I should let you get up to the house. I'm sure you're anxious to see *Mamm* and *Dat*."

"You're not staying?"

"Nah, me and the guys are working a construction job and we need to finish. *Dat* said you were coming home, so I wanted to swing by and say hi."

"*Denki* for coming."

Ephraim nodded. "Welcome home, *bruder*."

Denki, Gott. Ach, but he served a *gut gut Gott*!

THIRTY-SEVEN

*J*acob watched as Ephraim left with his motley crew. He and the older *kinner* continued to the house on foot, while Rachel, Dinah, and the two youngest *bopplin* rode up to the house in the van. Jacob's troop arrived just after Rachel disembarked with the *boppli*.

He grasped her hand and bent to kiss her cheek. "You ready?"

Her countenance beamed like rays of sunshine bursting through the trees lining their property. "*Jah*, very."

Mamm flew out of the house and nearly crashed into Jacob the way Ephraim had, but with less force. "*Sohn*, I'm so glad you've *kumm* home!" She hugged him briefly, then pulled back. "*Ach*, look at that full beard. You are almost as handsome as your *dat*."

Jacob shared glances with Rachel.

"And is this your beautiful *fraa*?" *Mamm's* smile widened. "Rachel, right?"

"*Ach, jah*. This is my beloved." Jacob brought her forward.

Mamm wrapped Rachel in a welcoming embrace. "It's *gut* to have you both home. Welcome, Rachel."

"*Denki*." Tears shimmered in Rachel's eyes. "It's *gut* to be here. I didn't realize it would look like this. *Ach*, it's *wunderbaar*!"

Mamm's arm linked with Rachel's elbow like they were already best friends. "You know, that's what I thought when I first met Isaac. Right here in this very spot. The day I fell in love. Just wait until you see all the property."

Mamm winked at him. "I'm sure Jacob will be happy to give you the grand tour."

"I'll take her everywhere. After we rest a bit. I'm sure Rachel's tired."

"Now, let me take a look at these *grossbopplin*! *Ach*, Jacob, they are *schee*. Let's see if I can remember…this *boppli* is Zeb, right?"

Rachel nodded. "Would you like to hold him?"

"I'd love to." She nestled the little one close to her chest. "*Ach*, he's a little doll."

"*Jah*, he is." Rachel grinned.

Mamm looked up at the other *kinner*. "And which of you *buwe* is the oldest."

"I am," Reuben declared.

"You must be Reuben. Then, let's see. Simeon. Levi. Judah."

Each of the boys nodded as she said their name. She promptly shook their hands.

"And this sweet princess must be Dinah." *Mamm* pulled his only *dochder* into a hug. "You and I are going to have a lot of fun. I never had a little girl."

Dinah beamed.

"And these younger *buwe* must be Dan, Gad, and Ash." She greeted the younger boys. "And I bet these *kinner* would love to have a cookie or two."

The kids exploded in excitement. Jacob chuckled. "I would like a cookie or two."

"I wanna see my room!" Dan exclaimed.

"*Kumm*, let's all go inside." *Mamm* suggested.

Jacob touched her shoulder. "Where's *Dat*?" He thought he might be out there to greet him and his family. Disappointment turned his lips down.

"*Ach*, I told you he's been weak lately. I wouldn't let him *kumm* outside. He's sitting on the couch waiting for you." She shook her head. "He must not be feeling *gut*, because I didn't think I'd be able to keep him in the house. All he's been talking about is Jacob coming home."

That lifted Jacob's spirits. So *Dat wasn't* indifferent to his return. "Let's go say hello, then."

They all followed *Mamm* into the house. Jacob draped his arm around Rachel's shoulders. *Ach*, he couldn't wait to show her everything.

Dat apparently had fallen asleep on the couch. *Mamm* shook his shoulder. "Isaac, Jacob's family is here."

Dat's eyes flew open. "Jacob?"

Jacob rounded the couch and planted himself next to his *vatter*. "Yep, it's me." He smiled, reached for *Dat*, and pulled him into a hug.

"*Ach*, you've grown into a man, *sohn*. And look at all these *kinner*."

Jacob rattled off their names in five seconds.

"You have some fine *kinner*, Jacob." His father smiled. "And I see you found yourself a beautiful *fraa*, just like your *mamm*."

Jacob pulled Rachel near. "This is *mei fraa*, Rachel."

"It's a pleasure to meet you both." Rachel looked to *Mamm* and *Dat*. "Jacob speaks very highly of you. I couldn't wait to meet you."

Ach, but she was a blessing from *Der Herr* indeed. His love for her would never die.

Mamm brought out the plate of cookies and called the *kinner* to the table. They all took a seat. *Mamm* gave them each a glass of goat milk too. Not everyone cared for the strong taste, but Jacob had grown up on it and came to appreciate it. Many times he'd heard the verse from Proverbs twenty-seven about having goat milk.

"Your *vatter* and I have since relocated downstairs, so the master bedroom is all yours," *Mamm* said, bringing a plate of cookies for Jacob, Rachel, and *Dat*.

"*Ach*, I want to show Rachel." Jacob beamed. "Do you two mind watching the *kinner*?"

"*Ach*, we'd love to. I know your *vatter* is dying to hold this *boppli*."

Jacob stood and reached his hand toward Rachel. "*Kumm, fraa*."

He led the way up the staircase to the open loft. Rachel turned around and surveyed the activity below them. They had a full view of the large living area and the dining room and kitchen.

"*Kumm*." Jacob opened the double doors to the bedroom. "This is our bedroom."

"*Ach*, Jacob." She gasped. Tears filled her eyes. "It's *wunderbaar*."

She went to the bed, admiring the large wooden posts. Then she jumped on the bed, spread out her arms, and sighed. "This is the best."

He joined her. They laid down, staring up at the ceiling.

She turned on her side, propping her head on her

hand. "You didn't tell me you were wealthy, Jacob."

"*We* are wealthy." He shrugged. "And you never asked."

"I can't believe all this is ours! *Ach*, Jacob, I feel like one of those princesses in a fairy tale."

"You are my princess, Mrs. King." He brought her hand to his lips and kissed it.

"It's all so *schee*, I don't even know what to say."

"So you're happy?"

"So, so happy." She kissed him with her smiling lips. "Can you believe we're married? And we have our own place? It was a dream I thought might never come true. And now it's here."

He kissed her back, but forced himself to stop before they got carried away. "None of that yet. I still have much to show you."

"There's more?" Her eyes widened.

He hopped off the bed and reached for her hand. "*Kumm, lieb.*"

He pulled her to a set of double doors, then opened them.

"*Ach*, Jacob!" Her hand flew to her lips and tears surfaced in her eyes. "It's so…so beautiful. We have our own porch?"

He chuckled. "It's called a balcony."

"We can come out here and watch the stars twinkle at night."

"Or you can put on your bathing suit and sit out in the sun." His grin stretched wide, knowing it would get a rise out of her.

She lightly punched his arm. "Jacob! *Ach*, you know I would never do that."

His mouth curled up into a half-smile and he raised his eyebrows. "I wouldn't mind."

She shook her head. "*Nee*. I would never."

"Maybe not here. But tomorrow I'll show you a place where you can wear your bathing suit."

"For real?" *Ach*, he'd never tire of seeing the smile on her face.

"Yep. Tomorrow."

❧

Rachel grinned as Jacob led her by the hand. She had no idea where he was taking her to. He'd just said he had something to show her. All these new adventures were so exciting. It almost seemed like she and Jacob were on a honeymoon without the *kinner* present. Having occasional babysitters would be nice.

"Don't worry about the *kinner*. *Mamm* said they will be just fine. She has them working on a project."

"A project?"

"*Jah*. They're making their own candles. Well, the older ones are. But the *boppli* will be asleep for another hour at least and *Mamm's* got the two littlest ones occupied in a playpen in the kitchen."

"Sounds like she has everything under control."

"She sure does. I think *Mamm* would have liked to have more *kinner*, if she could. But *Der Herr* only blessed her with twin *buwe*."

Rachel frowned. "I know how she feels."

Jacob tightened his grip on her hand and glanced at her. "You know, the doctors said my *mamm* couldn't have *kinner* either."

"Really? Then…what happened?"

"*Dat* prayed."

"That's it?"

He nodded.

"Do you think maybe he would pray for a *boppli* for me?"

"You mean *for us*."

"*Jah*." She frowned. "It just…it seemed so easy for Leah. I mean, you didn't do anything different with her, did you?"

He frowned. "What do you mean?"

"I mean, something different, something special to have a *boppli*."

"Do you think I'm *purposely* not helping you get in

the *familye* way?" Frustration simmered in his tone.

She shrugged, fighting back her tears of jealousy.

"*Lieb*." His tone gentled. "I loved your *schweschder* the same way I love you. Well, physically speaking. There's not a thing I do different that I can think of."

"Maybe there are no *bopplin* left for me." She swallowed hard.

"*Ach*, Rachel. These things are not something we can control. It's not up to us whether you have a *boppli* or not. But I will pray for it, if that's what you want. We could ask *Dat* too."

"*Ach*, Jacob, wouldn't it be *wunderbaar* to have our own *bopplin*?"

"I'd love to have a *boppli* with you. I can only imagine how beautiful he or she will be if they look anything like their *mamm*."

"Or their *dat*."

He shook his head in denial.

"Where are we going again?" She ducked her head under a tree branch and attempted to stay on the cleared path along the wooded trail.

"Our favorite spot. Just wait until you see it. I'm sure you will love it." He grinned. "Take a deep breath."

They were now ensconced in a utopia of lush greenery. "*Ach*, it smells so sweet!"

"Okay, I want you to close your eyes and take my hand."

"Okay." She held her hand out to him and allowed him to lead her.

"It's okay, I won't let you fall. I'll catch you if you stumble."

She heard the sound of something. Was it a stream? *Nee*, she felt mist.

"Alright. Open your eyes."

They'd come to a clearing. A lovely waterfall cascaded into a small pool right in front of her eyes. "Jacob! *Ach*, Jacob. This is like paradise."

"*Sehr schee*, ain't so?"

"Wonderful *schee*. *Ach,* Jacob. Thank you for bringing me here." She closed her eyes and listened to the rushing water, letting the mist caress her face. "*Ach*, this place makes my heart feel better. It's like medicine for my soul."

"This is where *Mamm* and *Dat* shared their very first real kiss."

"How romantic."

"We sometimes would come and swim in the pool. Maybe you and I can come out here alone again and…"

Her heart sped up. *Ach*, it would be wonderful and dangerous to come out here and swim with Jacob. She'd never swam with *buwe* present growing up. But, of course, she and Jacob were married so…

"*Jah*." She tucked her bottom lip under her teeth. "It sounds romantic."

"Well, my *Dat* is definitely the king when it comes to romance."

She giggled. "What do you mean?"

"He bought *Mamm* a ring before they married. Before they even met, actually."

"But she didn't wear it?"

"Maybe when no one was watching." He winked. "I'll have to show it to you sometime."

"I'd like that." She went and sat down on a fallen log. "But for now, I just want to sit here and enjoy *Gott's* beauty."

"And maybe a few kisses?" His tone was pleading.

She couldn't mask her smile. *Ach*, she loved being married to Jacob King! "And maybe a few kisses."

EPILOGUE

Five years later…

"It's a boy!" the midwife exclaimed. "Congratulations, you two."

Jacob waited patiently while the midwife completed her duties. He bent down and kissed Rachel's forehead. "We have a son, *lieb*."

He stretched his arms out and the midwife placed his brand-new *boppli* in them. *Ach*, he was tiny. Precious.

He brought the *boppli* close for his *fraa* to see.

"A son?" Tears flowed down Rachel's cheeks. "I have a *boppli*, Jacob. *Der Herr* gave me a *boppli*."

"Us. He gave *us* a *boppli*." He reminded her. "You had help making him, remember? Don't you go taking all the credit." He teased.

"*Jah, our boppli*." Her eyes shown with love.

"He looks right *gut* too." Jacob knew he must be beaming from ear to ear. Had he ever been this happy when the other *kinner* were born? "To share a child with the woman I love more than anything is nearly too much for my heart to handle."

"May we call him Joseph?"

"Joseph sounds like a wonderful *gut* name. There's something special about this *bu*, I can feel it." Jacob couldn't tamper his excitement.

"You think *Der Herr* might call him to His service?"

Jacob shrugged. "Don't know. I just know he's extra special. We've waited a long time for him, *jah*?"

"Too long. But I will cherish him anyhow. He was worth the wait."

"We will be thankful for *Der Herr's* provision. He knows exactly what we need and precisely when we need it. Joseph was born now, at this moment in time, for a purpose that only *Der Herr* knows."

"You are right, Jacob, my beloved."

"Would you like to hold him now?"

"*Jah*, please." She stretched her arms out to receive the bundle of joy. She gazed down at the wonderful *gut* blessing they'd created together with *Gott's* help. "He's precious. So small."

"What do you think his *brieder* and *schweschder* will say?" Jacob frowned. Hopefully the *kinner* wouldn't be jealous of their new little *bruder*. Especially since he was a half-brother to them. He'd have to be extra cautious.

"They will love him just as well as we do, I suppose. Do you think we should call them in now?"

"*Nee*. Let's enjoy this sweet one to ourselves just a few moments longer." Jacob stroked the *boppli's* head. "He is a fine *bu*. A fine *bu*."

"*Jah*, he is." Happy tears ran down his *fraa's* cheeks. "He is our son, Jacob."

He bent down and kissed her lips. "That's right, *our* son."

THE END

THE END

Dear Reader,

I hope you've enjoyed each book in this series!

This particular book was a little more challenging to write because, as you know, in the Biblical story, Jacob was married to both Rachel and Leah at the same time. And then there were their handmaids too!

Ach, could you imagine being in a situation like the one in this story? Jacob and Rachel and Leah's story? Rachel, having the man she loved ripped from her arms. Leah, being pressured to marry a man she knew didn't love her, and really didn't even know, practically a stranger. And poor Jacob, stuck in the middle of two sisters and an overbearing father-in-law, just trying to do the right thing and please everyone at the same time. Yet, not wanting to lose his beloved to someone else.

What a mess! But in the end, God worked everything out for His good.

And isn't that what He does with *our* lives? Sometimes we get ourselves into messes. And some of our messes can be really ugly! But God...

God is so good.

No matter where you are in your life right now, whether things are wonderful or you're in the middle of one of those messes, you can know that if you are a child of God, He's got you in His hands. If you need help, just ask Him. If all is well, thank Him. If all is not well, still thank Him. Because He *will* see you through.

If you're not a child of God, you can change that today. Right now. How, you ask? Just call out to Him. Pray. Tell God you need Him and you want Him in your life. He honors the prayer that's been spoken from the heart. He wants to be your Heavenly Father. He wants to bless you with good things. But the most wonderful part about being His child is knowing that a forever home awaits you in Heaven—a home with your Heavenly Father.

Thank you once again for reading. I pray the story touched your heart.

To GOD be the glory!

Blessings,
Jennifer Spredemann
Heart-Touching Amish Fiction

P.S. If you've enjoyed this book (or any of my books, for that matter) please tell your Amish fiction-reading friends. Also, it would be a *great blessing* to me if you'd consider leaving a review. <3

Thanks for reading!

To find out more about Jennifer Spredemann, join my email list, or purchase other books, please visit me at www.jenniferspredemann.com. My books are available in Paperback, eBook, and Audiobook formats. You may also follow Author Jennifer Spredemann on Facebook, Pinterest, Twitter, BookBub, Amazon, and Goodreads.

Questions and comments are always welcome. Feel free to email the author at jebspredemann@gmail.com.

Discussion Questions

1. Isaac and Rebekah had unwittingly pitted their sons against each other by choosing favorites. Can you relate to this in your own life?

2. Jacob and Ephraim's childhood had been filled with insecurity and strife, even though they grew up with loving, well-intentioned parents. Have you experienced sibling rivalry?

3. We see in the Bible that sin can easily take a hold of our hearts. It can turn us against others and quickly get out of hand, even to the point of murder, as in the stories of Cain and Abel, and Jacob and Esau. This is why it is important to confess and forsake our sin. Have you ever harbored bitterness, jealousy, or hatred in your heart? Did you act on those emotions? What did you do (or could you have done) to prevent those feelings from getting out of hand?

4. Jacob had to move away to keep himself safe. Have you ever had to flee for your life? How did it work out in the end?

5. Have you read the Old Testament Bible story of Esau, Jacob, Rachel, and Leah? What are your thoughts on it?

6. One thing I enjoy about Biblical fiction is that it helps the true Biblical characters seem more real to me, even though I know a fictional story isn't real. Do you find that true for yourself as well?

7. In the story, each person seems to have their own reasons for doing what they do. (i.e. Marlin looking out for his daughters' welfare) Does understanding where they are coming from help you sympathize with them?

8. What would you have done if you were in Jacob's shoes? Leah's? Rachel's?

9. Jacob had been taught in his church that being a '*gut* Amish man' would influence his eternal home. Larry showed him that being Amish (or any other religion) had nothing to do with salvation. It is Christ alone whom our salvation rests upon. Are you sure of your eternal destination?

10. Rachel questioned her church's belief that death was *Gott's* will. Do you believe that death is God's will? Why or why not?

11. What was your favorite part of *An Amish Deception*, and why?

12. What lessons can you take from Jacob's story? How can you apply it to your own life?

A SPECIAL THANK YOU

I'd like to take this time to thank everyone that had any involvement in this book and its production, including my Mom and Dad, who have always been supportive of my writing, my longsuffering Family—especially my handsome, encouraging Hubby, my Amish and former-Amish friends who have helped immensely in my understanding of the Amish ways, my supportive Pastor and Church family, my Proofreaders, my Editor, my CIA Facebook author friends who have been a tremendous help, my wonderful Readers who buy, read, offer great input, and leave encouraging reviews and emails, my awesome Street Team who, I'm confident, will 'Sprede the Word' about my books! And last, but certainly not least, I'd like to thank my *Precious LORD and SAVIOUR JESUS CHRIST*, for without Him, none of this would have been possible!